Who Killed
Christopher Goodman?

Who Killed
Christopher Goodman?

·ALLAN WOLF·

Based on a true crime

CANDLEWICK PRESS

First U.S. paperback edition 2019

Library of Congress Catalog Card Number 2017931943
ISBN 978-0-7636-5613-3 (hardcover)
ISBN 978-1-5362-0877-1 (paperback)

21 22 23 24 25 TRC 10 9 8 7 6 5 4 3 2

Printed in Eagan, MN, U.S.A.

This book was typeset in PT Serif.

Candlewick Press
99 Dover Street
Somerville, Massachusetts 02144

visit us at www.candlewick.com

For Ed

Your resonance lingered in lions and rocks

and in the trees and birds. There you are singing still.

Rainer Maria Rilke from *Sonnets to Orpheus*

· VOICES ·

David Oscar "Doc" Chestnut
·
The Sleepwalker

Leonard Pelf
·
The Runaway

Scott "Squib" Kaplan
·
The Genius

Hunger McCoy
·
The Good Ol' Boy

Hazel Turner
·
The Farm Girl

Mildred Penny
·
The Stamp Collector

For the teenagers of Goldsburg High School, the summer of 1979 was marching-band practice and football practice and cross-country practice and part-time jobs. It was a single-screen theater downtown, the Lyric, playing a new movie called *Alien*. It was a bookstore, a music store, and a hardware store. It was the College Inn Diner, where you could get breakfast or lunch. And Carol Lee's, where you could get a donut. And it was funky Mr. Fooz, where you could play pool, foosball, pinball, video games, eat pizzas and subs, or just hang out in the air-conditioning. Dave's Dawgs was across the street from Mr. Fooz. And, well . . . that was about it.

On summer weekends in 1979, most teenagers would pile into whatever car or truck they could find and make the twenty-mile drive out of town to McCoy Falls on the New River. Here the young people would cover the rocks like a rookery of sea lions.

The largest and highest of these river rocks was called the Jump. Against this school bus–size monolith the New River current fought, foamed, and finally divided. The river had been compromising this way for centuries, digging out the bed of the downstream side, forming a swimming hole some fifteen feet deep.

A hundred yards downstream was a little beach, more mud than sand. And at the far end of this beach stood a rusty old mailbox attached to a post at the river's edge. Inside the mailbox was a small pad of notepaper. And a pencil with the eraser apparently chewed off. On the side of the mailbox, in crude lettering, were the words *Wishes, Hopes, and Dreams*.

According to local lore, any wishes left in the box would be granted, yearnings would be heard, and prayers would be answered. The New River Mailbox had been there as long as anyone could remember. Somebody tended it, but no one knew who. Any scrap of paper placed in that mailbox was gone the next day.

In 1979, Goldsburg, Virginia was a bustling college town—at least during the school year. But whenever the college closed its doors for the summer, things got bleak and slow. To keep the locals from going nuts—and the downtown shops from going broke—the Goldsburg Merchants' Association had created the Deadwood Days street festival, held annually during the first full weekend in August. Named after Deadwood, South Dakota, the wild west–themed affair was not to be missed. In 1979, for the students at Goldsburg High School, Deadwood Days was the highlight of a long, dull summer. It featured food and live music. Craft booths. A petting zoo. A one-mile road race. Stagecoach rides. Even fake gunfights.

•1•

ELEPHANT BELLS

The Morning After
Deadwood Days

Doc Chestnut • *The Sleepwalker*

The morning after Deadwood Days, like every other morning, I rose before sunup to deliver forty-five copies of the *Goldsburg News Messenger*. Usually the task was mindless and relaxing. Usually, by the end of these long quiet bike rides my head would be as empty as the streets. But that day, the morning after Deadwood Days, my mind was a jumble of events from the night before. The night had started off so well. How had it ended so badly?

My last delivery, as always, was the large new house just across the street and a couple doors down. I tossed the folded paper onto the wooden porch with a loud *pop,* like a firecracker. This was the home of Christopher Goodman. Just a few hours before, I had pointed out the house to Mildred Penny, the girl of my dreams.

Christopher Goodman. Mildred Penny. More clatter in my head.

"David Oscar Chestnut," I said to myself, "you are an idiot beyond measure!"

My papers were delivered by nine a.m. My mind grew calmer. I changed into running shorts and did warm-up stretches on the driveway as I waited for my friend Squib. At nine-thirty a.m., like clockwork, Squib pulled up to the curb in a chugging ice cream truck, huge and pink, with pictures of ice cream bars and Popsicles of every description. Even with its huge loud speaker turned off, I could still hear the tune "Pop Goes the Weasel" in my head. This had been Squib's only mode of transportation all summer long.

He bounded out of the ice cream truck onto the sidewalk, like Tigger in *Winnie-the-Pooh*. Huge running shorts. Tall white socks. Skinny white legs. Knobby knees. Running shoes like boats. He did a shuffling dance, up and down the length of the van.

"This step is the latest craze," he said, too wide awake as usual. "I call it the Squib!"

"I've seen it before, you weirdo," I said. "You've been doing it since first grade."

We had been meeting like this almost every morning all summer, training for cross-country in the fall.

From here Squib and I set out on a special eight-mile loop, what our coach whimsically referred to as LSD—long slow distance. Our route began along Palmer Drive, separating the old neighborhood (my side) from the new-built, and much nicer, houses across the street. As we jogged past the newest and nicest of these homes, the Goodman house, I looked away. That noise in my head rustled back to life like birds in a chimney.

"...and are you even listening to me?" said Squib, punching my arm.

"Yes. Sure," I said, startled. "I mean, no. Actually, no."

"I was saying," Squib went on, "that I have calculated *fssst* the number of steps in a typical eight-mile run."

I should mention that, due to Tourette syndrome, Squib's normal talking voice was punctuated with odd little vocal tics. The latest tic sounded something like a convulsive sneeze.

I said, "You counted your steps?"

"Yes," he said. "Of course, I didn't actually count my own steps for eight miles. I simply *fssst* counted them during a four-hundred-and-forty-yard lap around the high school track and then extrapolated . . ."

As Squib talked, we jogged a mile more on Palmer. Turned left on Country Club. Left onto Main. Past the Bonanza Steak House. Past Gables Shopping Center. Past the Mic-or-Mac Grocery where I'd nearly been arrested for robbery just two weeks before (more on that later). We passed the Hop-In convenience store that stocked *Playboy* and *Penthouse* on their shelves in back. And took a left down Ellett Valley Road. Past quiet houses. The sun now high. Past a little white church.

And all the while, Squib talked and talked. And all the while the events of the night before haunted me. It had been one of the most exhilarating nights of my sleepwalking life, until I ruined it by doing something stupid.

"Oh my God!" said Squib as he came to a sudden halt.

There on the road's shoulder. A dark shape near the top of a shallow embankment. Lying still on the ground.

"What is it?" I said.

It was a kid. About my own age. The air around him was thick with buzzing bottle flies. Insects crawled over his sandaled feet. Mud splattered the cuffs of his wide bell-bottom pants.

"Oh my God! *Fssst.* Oh my God," said Squib. "Doc! Look at his bell-bottoms. Look at his *fssst* bell-bottoms."

The bell-bottoms were wide, with an extra triangle of fabric, a little American flag, sewn into them to make them even wider. Only one kid in all of Goldsburg wore pants like that.

Christopher Goodman.

Professor's Son, 17, Slain

GOLDSBURG—Two boys jogging along Ellett Valley Road found the body of 17-year-old Christopher Charles Goodman about 11:00 a.m. Sunday, a mile south of Goldsburg city limits, police said.

Deputy chief medical examiner for Western Virginia, Dr. Max Butterworth, said that Goodman had been dead since Saturday night. Butterworth said the boy apparently died from a gunshot wound to the head. He declined to say what type of weapon had been used.

Goodman was last seen alive Saturday evening at Deadwood Days, Goldsburg's cowboy-themed street festival. An officer at the scene stated that the motive appeared to be auto theft but declined to give more details. An investigation is underway.

Goodman would have been a senior at Goldsburg High School. He is survived by his parents, Professor Randall E. and Mrs. Evelyn D. Goodman, and an older sister, Laura.

The family has asked that memorial donations be made to the Goldsburg High School Band.

•2•

WHO WAS CHRISTOPHER GOODMAN?

**Four Weeks
After
Deadwood Days**

WRITING ASSIGNMENT
Memorial Poem For Christopher Goodman

Write a memorial poem about Christopher Goodman
using iambic pentameter and A/B/A/B rhyme.
Don't worry if you didn't know him very well.
Let your emotions and memories run free
within the confines of the prescribed form!

Include all pre-writing in your process journal.

Due Date: September 11

Four weeks after Deadwood Days, classes resumed at Goldsburg High School. On the first day back, homeroom lists had been posted in the lunchroom with Christopher's name crossed through:

Goodman, Christopher Charles

The sight of it made my stomach turn.

There had been no funeral. No memorial service. There was no grave to visit. Goodman's parents had the body cremated. No word of what became of the ashes. One day he was there. The next day he was gone.

My second-period class was officially named Advanced Literacy Studies: Creative Writing, called ALS for short—just like Lou Gehrig's disease. There were only, maybe, a dozen students in all. Squib was there. And Mildred Penny, with whom I was secretly in love. And Hazel Turner, who worked with Mildred Penny at the College Inn Diner. And Hunger McCoy, who was a member of a group of beefy good-ol'-boy football players who called themselves the Bronco Brothers. There were others, but they aren't important to the story.

When our teacher, Mrs. Maybury, told us that we were going to write about Christopher Goodman, I thought I might be sick.

"In sad times like these," said Mrs. Maybury, "John Keats reminds us that, ay, in the very temple of delight, veiled melancholy has her sovereign shrine." She held a hand to her heart. "I want you to embrace the beauty of your sorrow! Mine your

9

grief for literary gems!" She paused for effect. "Write, write, write!"

Someone raised her hand and asked, "Who *was* Christopher Goodman? I mean, I know he was killed and all. But I'm not really sure I know who he *was*."

As all of this was going on I shifted in my seat. I looked first at Squib, then Hunger, then Penny, then Hazel. They were all doing the same, the five of us, shooting each other glances like twitchy birds.

It was pretty obvious that few people in the class had really known Christopher Goodman that well. Some hadn't known him at all. I *did* know one thing for sure. And Squib knew it, too. And Mildred Penny knew. And Hazel Turner. And Hunger McCoy.

We had all been together at Deadwood Days. The night Christopher Goodman died.

CENTRAL STATE HOSPITAL
ADOLESCENT UNIT
PSYCHOLOGICAL EVALUATION

EVALUATION DATE: 9/4/1979
NAME: Leonard Pelf
DATE OF BIRTH: 10/11/63
AGE: 15
CASE NO. 89315

TEST BEHAVIOR AND OBSERVATIONS:

Leonard's responses to the Rorschach inkblots (RI) suggest that no psychosis or organicity is present. He appears constricted cognitively, which may reflect low intellectual functioning. Leonard may ignore his emotions, which eventually culminates in his acting them out at later times. It appears that the patient has difficulty with authority figures. He may be immature and impulsive in his behavior, and he seems to disregard other people. He says that he "feels bad" about what happened; however, when reporting this he speaks in a matter-of-fact way. Finally, Leonard may be lackadaisical in his approach to life.

> VERNON VICTOR, Ph.D.
> PSYCHOLOGIST/SUPERVISOR
> September 4, 1979

Leonard Pelf • *The Runaway*

To see if I was crazy or not,
my court-appointed headshrinker
shows me a bunch of ink splotches
and asks me to make sense of them.
I play along best as I can,
but afterward I just feel like a fool.

I say, "That there ink splotch looks like
a little bug-eyed Chihuahua."
I say, "That there ink splotch looks like
the General Lee in midair jumping up over a creek."
But that must've been the wrong answer cause
he says, "I need you to be serious now, Leonard."

And I want to say, *I am being serious.*
I want to say, *I never joke about* Dukes of Hazzard.
I want to say, *The General Lee is an awesome car.*
But instead I say, "Okay, I guess I don't see nothin'."

The next splotch looks like Daisy Duke's ass
but I can't exactly tell him *that,* can I?
Instead, I just say, "I don't know."

And, "Maybe."

And, "I guess so."

And, "I don't see nothin'."

And that head-shrinker writes it all down
like I just told him my whole life story.

Doc Chestnut • *The Sleepwalker*

I was a sleepwalker. When I was a very small child, my parents would find me sleepwalking all over the house like a preschool zombie. I would scribble on the coffee table or open up the fridge to take a pee. I got older, and my walks became more dangerous. My father once stopped me from starting up the car. My mother smelled smoke and discovered me cooking spaghetti, no water in the pot.

One night, I woke up standing inside the shell of a half-completed house. The construction site was located just across the street in what had once been an empty field. Before being sold off to developers, this field witnessed dirt-bike races, fireworks displays, BB gun wars, snow forts, and sleds. Poisonous milkweed grew in thick head-high hedges, always surrounded by clouds of Monarch butterflies. We harvested praying mantis oothecae from the limbs of tall sumac trees and hid among the bitter crimson berries, where we melted our eyelashes lighting cigarette butts. We gaped, wide-eyed, at *Playboy* and *Penthouse* and argued the pros and cons of breast size, hair color, and body type.

But the field dissolved in my sleepwalking dream, and I woke to the smell of sawdust and cement, in the unfinished house that would eventually be Christopher Goodman's home.

I had thought that empty field would be there forever. Then one night I woke up and found myself in the dark, half-naked and surrounded by change. I would sleepwalk less and less as I got older. But sometimes, even when I was awake, I still felt half-asleep. As if I was trapped inside a dream.

Many times when I saw Christopher Goodman, the memory of the fading field and the Goodmans' rising skeleton house would play in my mind.

•3•

A BOSS RIDE

Four Weeks
Before
Deadwood Days

After Doc and I finished our morning run, I stocked the ding-a-ling truck with bomb pops, ice cream sandwiches, Nutty Buddies, fudge bars, push-ups, snowballs, creamsicles, Pink Panthers, Mickeys, Tweeties, Choco-Crunches, and Big Dippers. We called it a ding-a-ling truck which makes it sound tiny and cute, but Kaplan's Ice Cream Van was anything but tiny. It was a tall GMC step van that my Uncle Hiram had modified himself, with an awning and a service window on the passenger side, and three freezers with sliding glass tops, all powered by a noisy gas generator made from an old VW engine that hung off the back.

When my sister left for college, Uncle Hiram said, "I need you to fill your sister's shoes." I said, "But she doesn't *wear* shoes. *Fssst.* She wears flip-flops and a bikini top!" As soon as I took over, profits dropped due to the loss of my sister's customer base of horny male teenagers. But the money was still pretty good, and Uncle Hiram let me keep the van in case I had a big date. (Which was never).

I pressed my foot to the clutch, turned the key, and my boss ride came to life. Then I flipped a red switch under the dash. "Pop Goes the Weasel" blasted from the ancient loudspeaker mounted on the roof. Doc Chestnut wasn't with me. He used to ride along. But not so much anymore. Was he too embarrassed? Maybe. Or maybe it was because "Pop Goes the Weasel" would play every thirty seconds, which means hearing "Pop Goes the Weasel" exactly six hundred times over the course of a typical five-hour shift.

Leonard Pelf • *The Runaway*

I hear "Pop Goes the Weasel"
getting louder and louder.
Scrabbles, Mr. and Mrs. G's bug-eyed dog,
yaps as the ice cream truck goes by.
Then it's gone, headed toward the graveyard.
And I'm stuck here helping Mr. G wash his big car.

"Be careful not to wash off the bumper sticker," says Mr. G.
The sticker says JESUS IS MY CO-PILOT.
Bo and Luke Duke would not approve.
Mr. G plays redneck gospel songs on the cassette deck.
It's all *damnation this* and *salvation that.*
And he gives me advice like he thinks he owns me,
like he's some sort of father figure.

He says, "The Devil is an arsonist, kiddo.
He sets fires for the pure hell of it.
Then he just walks away.
The Devil leaves it up to *you*
to get the hell outta that burnin' house.
God ain't gonna pull you out;
Jesus ain't gonna pull you out neither;
you gotta escape all on your own!"

I think, *If the devil sets* my *house on fire*
I'll rescue all the kids, put out the fire,
and then I'll kick the devil's ass.

But I don't say it out loud.
Instead I say, "Can you teach me how to drive?"
Mr. G is all big smiles and says,
"Sure, kiddo, you want me to teach you to drive?"

No, I think. *What I really want is to take your car
and get the hell outta here and go to Hollywood.*

But I don't say that out loud, neither.
Instead I smile. Just like Momma taught me.

Instead I say, "Yes sir, Mr. G. That'd be real nice."

My friend Wayne drives a 1977 charcoal gray Ford Bronco Ranger with a 302 V-8 and a convertible top. That's why me and my buddies are called the Bronco Brothers. We were on our way from football practice down to the river with two coolers in the back. One cooler was for PBR and one cooler was for just in case I seen a good specimen on the road. Wayne was behind the wheel. I rode shotgun, like always. Eddie and Wesley were on the bench in the back.

The boys know to keep an eye out for any roadkill with potential.

"Remember fellas," I said. "It's gotta be pretty fresh and not too flat."

"Why not just use a gun?" said Eddie, shouting from the back.

"That's not the point, lunkhead," I said, shouting even louder.

Between work, football practice, and taxidermy, I didn't get much time to blow off steam. For some reason, with Mom so sick, I couldn't pick up the guitar. Mostly she slept all the time, and just being in the quiet house made me wanna scream.

But it was hard to be sad when the Bronco Brothers were around. Wesley and Eddie and Wayne were all lunkheads. And I guess I was a lunkhead too, but there you go.

In the backseat, Eddie and Wesley began a burping contest. We were rounding a really sharp curve on East Roanoke Street when out of nowhere comes this Chevy Impala, on *our* side of the double yellow line! Wayne jerked the wheel hard and ran the

Bronco off the road. And I felt a big THUNK as the front end ran up and over a log.

I turned my head just in time to see the back bumper of that Chevy disappear around the curve, but not before I caught a glimpse of the bumper sticker:

JESUS IS MY CO-PILOT

"Asshole!" yelled Eddie.

"Chickenshit Chevy!" yelled Wesley.

"I spilt my beer!" yelled Wayne.

But the Chevy was gone and the Bronco was left nose-up on a log, the front tires spinning, a good two feet off the ground!

We were in a no-win situation. The Bronco wasn't about to budge as long as the log was there. And we couldn't move the log with the Bronco on top of it. All four of us ducked our heads under the truck, trying to figure a way out.

"What about the winch?" said Eddie.

"You busted it trying to pull down the Radford High School bleachers. Remember?" said Wayne, opening a fresh beer.

"Oh, yeah," said Eddie.

"I told y'all that was a stupid idea," said Wesley.

"It was *your* idea to begin with!" said Wayne.

"Well, it woulda worked if y'all had just . . ."

As Wayne, Eddie, and Wesley argued, I saw a glimpse of white fur lying next to the log.

"Shut up," I said. "I think we hit something."

"Last year, I dated Hunger McCoy for about two minutes," I said. "It was a big mistake. It ruined our friendship."

The diner was empty except for me and the new girl, Mildred Penny. We were setting tables for the lunch rush.

"What happened?" asked Mildred.

"I called it off," I said. Then, "Are you really sorting those jelly packets by flavor?"

"By flavor *and* alphabetically," Mildred said. "Apple, blackberry, grape, orange, strawberry. What did Hunger do when you called it off?"

"Every time he saw me, he acted like his dog had just died," I said.

"Maybe his heart was broken," said Mildred.

I said, "If he truly cared about me, he would have hidden his feelings for the sake of our friendship." Why I was confiding all of this to Mildred Penny, I have no idea. I guess filling sugar dispensers just loosens my tongue.

"You can't expect him to hide his true feelings," said Mildred.

I said, "You sound like my mom. Even she thought I was too hard on him. Everybody said, 'Give the boy a break, farm girl. Who are *you* to be so picky? The boys certainly aren't lined up waitin' for *you!*'"

Mildred said, "I bet nobody really said that. That's a big fat lie."

"Look. I know who I am. And I know what I am. But why can't people mind their own business? I'm not a beauty queen, so everyone assumes I'm desperate. Then I have sex with one guy, one time, and suddenly I'm a slut. But if I turn guys *down*, I'm a dyke."

"I'm sure there's somebody out there for you," Mildred said.

"Oh, save it. I don't mind not having a line of boys waiting. I just don't want to be judged. Not that I really care. Anyway," I went on, "Hunger and I broke up. He's not a bad guy at all. The whole roadkill thing is sorta creepy, to be sure. But Hunger McCoy can sing *every* Hank Williams or Merle Haggard song ever written. Hunger McCoy can pick the dickens out of a guitar. And Hunger McCoy hates to see any animal suffer."

"Shut up," I told Wayne, Wesley, and Eddie. "I think we hit something." I moved some leaves to reveal a cat, white with mud-matted fur.

"She must've been hiding behind that log," said Wesley.

"Well, *that* was a mistake," laughed Wayne.

"Is it dead?" said Eddie.

"Hell yeah, it's dead, meathead," said Wayne. "We just ran over it with a Ford Bronco!"

Just then the cat's tail twitched.

"She's alive!" I said. As the cat's ribs rose with air, I could see her baggy belly and her swollen teats. She was a mother. Somewhere there were kittens.

The momma cat's side rose up two or three more times, as if she was trying to wake herself up. But the breaths were raggedy and out of time. Then she hissed a little and was still.

"It *was* alive," said Wesley, with a snort.

"Well, *there's* yer roadkill for the day, Hunger. And we killed it ourselves," said Wayne, throwing back his can of PBR.

I picked up the cat as gentle as I could and glared at Wayne.

"What?" said Wayne.

"Hey, Hunger," said Eddie. "You okay?"

"It's a mother cat," I said. "I just don't find dead mother cats all that entertaining, I guess."

"Sorry," said Eddie. "I'm sorry the cat is dead. It was that Chevy's fault."

"I don't give a crap about a dead cat," Wayne said, as I put the mother cat's limp body in the cooler. "What I care about is that the Bronco is bottomed out on a log. You lug nuts busted my winch. And that means the only thing we can do is lift up the chassis with two jacks, one on each side, so we can slide the log out."

"Where are we gonna get a second jack?" said Wesley.

At just that moment this orange Ford Maverick pulls up beside us, blaring Queen's "Bohemian Rhapsody." The window rolls down. The music dies. And it's Christopher Goodman leanin' over with his Beatles haircut and his yellow-tinted sunglasses.

And he says, "Looks like your Bronco needs a lift."

"You got a jack?" I said.

And he steps out of his car and walks around to the trunk. He's wearing sandals and enormous bell-bottoms. And as he opens the trunk, I say, "Nice pants, Flower Power." Eddie, Wes, and Wayne all laughed at that.

But cool as a cucumber, Christopher Goodman turns to us all and pauses a second. And then, with a completely serious face, he says, "Thanks, Hunger. I like your pants, too. Now *this* oughta do the trick."

All us Bronco Brothers gathered around the back of the Maverick to have a look. And that's when we discovered that Christopher Goodman kept a top-of-the-line three-ton steel hydraulic floor jack in his trunk.

Mildred Penny • *The Stamp Collector*

Of course I had *seen* Christopher Goodman at school during the year. And at band practice over the summer. He was hard to miss. He was the new kid from California. He was tall, thin, and tan. And in really great shape. He dressed different. He talked different. And he acted different. And yet he seemed comfortable in his skin.

But the first time Christopher Goodman came into the College Inn Diner, I was working a slow, solo shift—carefully filling napkin dispensers and saltshakers. Organizing the jelly packets into sets of apple butter, blackberry, grape, orange marmalade, and strawberry.

He chose a booth by the window and sat alone. I went over to take his order. I figured he knew me from band practice, but I wasn't prepared for what happened next.

"My name is Chris Goodman," he said, and he shook my hand as if he was genuinely glad to see me. And maybe he really *was*. "And you are Mildred Penny," he continued.

I wasn't sure how to answer. It wasn't really a question. It was just a statement: "You are Mildred Penny." As if he had just named me himself.

"So what can I get you?" I said, still feeling the warmth of his handshake.

He ordered hash browns with ketchup. And he had a notebook with *Very Clever Songs by Christopher Goodman* written on the cover in bold black letters.

After he left and I cleared his table, I noticed that Christopher

Goodman had mixed up the jelly packets. Orange mingled with grape. Grape was with strawberry. Apple butter was with black-berry. It was chaotic. And completely without order.

I left it that way.

Leonard Pelf • *The Runaway*

Mr. and Mrs. G's kitchen phone has a long cord,
long enough that I can sit in the pantry for privacy.
Scrabbles scratches at the door and I let him in.
I dial the house where my little sister lives.
And they tell me she's been moved.
But they won't tell me where to.
Won't give me a number or nothing.
So I call Miss Hanna, who says,
"I'm afraid it's the judge's court order.
To give your sister a clean break."
"A break from what?" I ask.

All the court does is break what's broken.
Why don't the courts and the cops
and the lawyers and the judges
and the counselors and the social workers
ever *fix* anything? They just break broken folks
into smaller and smaller pieces.

I hang up the phone and step into the kitchen with Scrabbles.
Mr. G is reading the *Goldsburg News Messenger*.
Mrs. G is cookin' sausage and singin' about Jesus.
"You weren't talking to Lance, were you, kiddo?" says Mr. G.
"No, sir," I say. "That was Miss Hanna."
"What were y'all talking about?" says Mrs. G.
"Nothing," I say. "Just stuff."

Mr. G says, "We'll enroll you in the high school come fall."
Mrs. G says, "Come get the mustard and biscuits!"
"Lance'll be a junior," I say.
"Not if he flunks out," says Mr. G.
"Now let's sit down and give thanks," says Mrs. G.

I smile like Momma taught me.
And "Yes, ma'am," I say.
We hold hands. There at the table.
Near the kitchen peg
where Mr. G has hung the car keys.
And those keys are the last thing I see
before we bow our heads to pray.

Me and Christopher Goodman and the other Bronco Brothers all bowed our heads to get a closer look. "Why do you have that huge car jack in your trunk?" I asked.

"It weighs about a hundred pounds," said Goodman. "It gives my car more traction in the snow."

"But it's August," I said.

"I know," said Goodman, "I just never got around to taking it out. I figure, why not leave it where it is?"

In less than an hour, we had freed the Bronco, and we all helped Goodman lift the heavy jack back into his trunk. Next to the jack was Goodman's trombone in its case. Next to the trombone was a nice radio cassette recorder.

"That's for recording bands live," he said. "I'm trying to put a band together myself."

"Y'all gonna play any Hank Williams?" Eddie asked.

"Maybe," said Goodman, "Right now we just have three trombones and a drummer."

"You're gonna play Hank Williams on the trombone?" said Wayne, laughing.

"Why not?" said Goodman.

"I do a little pickin' myself," I said.

"I know," said Goodman. "You sang 'Sweet Home Alabama' in the school talent show last year. You were great. Better than great, actually. And I saw the article in the paper—about you stuffing roadkill?"

"Oh, yeah, that," I said.

"Hunger is the Michelangelo of roadkill," laughed Eddie.

"We got a fresh dead cat on ice in the cooler," said Wayne. "You wanna see it?"

"Shut up, Wayne," I said.

Then Goodman said, "You ought to make that dead cat dance."

"Do what?" I said.

"Make the dead cat dance," Goodman said again. "Animals are always stuffed in natural, boring poses. Why not give them a chance to do something unusual? If you're going to pose the cat at all, why not pose the cat ... dancing."

Christopher Goodman did a little jig. Then he shook the hand of every Bronco Brother there, as if he was running for mayor or something. And then Christopher Goodman got into his orange Ford Maverick, and he drove away. "Bohemian Rhapsody" was blasting from the speakers as he rounded the corner and disappeared.

All us Bronco Brothers stood there watchin' him drive away.

"That is one weird dude," said Wayne, cracking open another PBR.

"You got *that* right," said Eddie.

"And those pants!" said Wesley.

"Make the dead cat dance," I said. "Not a bad idea."

Mildred Penny • *The Stamp Collector*

The bell jingled, and in waltzed Christopher Goodman, singing "Sweet Home Alabama" and carrying a trombone case. He had started to come by the diner every day. Sometimes alone, but today he was with two upperclassmen boys from the trombone section. When I walked up to take their order, Christopher smiled at me (he had this great smile) and introduced me to his friends. And his eyes . . . oh, yes. His eyes.

"Mildred Penny?" said Christopher. "Meet Tony and Mike. Tony and Mike, this is Mildred Penny. She is a master clarinetist."

"We know Mildred already, Chris," said Mike. "We're all in band together, remember?"

"Hello, Mildred," said Tony.

"But did you know," said Christopher, "that Mildred Penny also collects stamps?"

I gasped. "How do you know that?"

"It was written up in the high school yearbook," he said.

"How embarrassing," I said. I felt my face grow hot.

"Not at all, Mildred, my father is a philatelist himself."

"A philat—" I tripped over the word.

"Philatelist," Christopher repeated. "It means—"

"Oh, I know what the word means." I stopped him. "I'm just surprised to hear anyone *say* it."

I was thrilled. Just the sound of the word—philatelist, philatelist—made my pulse race. And from Christopher's lips, in particular, the word had an even more mystical shimmer.

"Philatelist," he said again. And again, "Philatelist."

"Dude," said Mike. "You are such a weirdo."

Then Christopher, stretching out the syllables like Silly Putty, said, "Phffffiiiillll-aaaaa-tuuuuh-liiiiisss-tuh!"

This may have been the very instant that I fell secretly in love with Christopher Goodman.

The bell jingled as Squib and I entered the College Inn Diner.

"What's up, Doc?!" It was Christopher Goodman, with Mike and Tony, two other members of the trombone section.

"Hey, Christopher," I said back. Christopher shook my hand.

"Hey, Squibster," said Christopher.

"Hey," said Squib, laughing, as Christopher shook his hand too.

Then Christopher shook Mike's and Tony's hands, for good measure.

Then he said, "The lovely and talented Mildred Penny will be your server today. But whatever you do, don't ask her about her stamp collection."

After the three boys had left, Squib and I took a seat near the window.

"That Christopher Goodman *fssst* is quite the hand-shaker," said Squib.

"Oh, did they already leave?" said Mildred Penny as she walked up to our table. "I was in the back."

She frowned as she looked toward the door where Christopher had been. She held an empty to-go box in her hands.

"Hey, Mildred," said Squib. "Christopher said not to ask you *fssst* about your stamp collection."

With her eyes still fixed on the door, Mildred answered, "Really?" And her lips formed into a slight smile.

"Squib!" I said. "He said *not* to ask."

"So, Mildred?" said Squib, undeterred. "Do you collect stamps *fssst* or what?"

"No. Not really," said Mildred, still looking at the door.

While Mildred was held in this momentary trance, I sensed an opportunity to connect. I said, "Stamp collecting seems like a thing to do." Mildred turned and looked at me, confused, as if she had forgotten I was even there. Our eyes met for a second.

Then she placed a tray of jelly packets on the table and pulled out a notepad.

She said, "Can I take your order?"

•4•

IT BEGINS LIKE A YAWN!

Three Weeks
Before
Deadwood Days

Leonard Pelf • *The Runaway*

My yawn turns into a heartburn beer burp.
That's my reflection in the bathroom mirror
brushing my morning beer breath teeth.
I remember helping my brother and sister brush.
I used to take care of all three of us.
I can take care of myself just fine.
Before going to the movies last night
me 'n' Lance drank Old Milwaukee.

Mrs. G says I'm movie-star handsome.
She says, "Maybe, Leonard. Maybe one day,
so long as God wills it, you'll be a star like Gene Autry."

But I'd rather be a star like Bo and Luke Duke,
or maybe Smokey and the Bandit.
Them actors all drive awesome cars.
And them actors all live in Hollywood.
They're all rich and they get laid.

I lived with Mrs. and Mr. G once before,
at a shelter where they was house parents.
I was maybe twelve years old then.
Now I'm fifteen. They all run together.
The birthdays I mean. And the homes. And the parents.

They all run.

I've been with Mr. and Mrs. G all summer now.
They say they want to adopt me.
I say, "What about my brother and sister?"
They got nothin' to say to that.
My bedroom has a ceiling fan that only stirs the heat hotter.
I put on my sleeveless AC/DC shirt.
Mr. and Mrs. G don't like it. They've said so.
Only eight in the morning,
and it's already hot as the devil's coffee.

I go to the kitchen and get me an ice cube,
to rub on the inside of my wrist to keep cool.
Momma taught me that. She taught me a lot.
Momma taught me how to smile, like I mean it.

Squib Kaplan • *The Genius*

Doc and I used to hang out a lot more than we do. When I was in elementary school I was the most popular kid in my class, even though I was smarter than anyone (including my teachers), and even though my vocal tics were a *lot* louder and more frequent. In fact, I sounded pretty much like a human pinball machine. The kids thought I was the coolest thing ever, especially the boys. And none of us really cared what the girls thought, because we were all just in fourth grade! Then middle school happened, and suddenly *everybody* cared what the girls thought. And everybody got tall and wide while I still just looked like the Wizard of Id. And my pinball-machine tics morphed into my present (and apparently less cool) bellowing/sneezing/whistling tics. Then high school happened and I realized that being smarter than *every*one (including your teachers) can be just as alienating as making weird Jabberwocky noises.

One early morning Christopher Goodman came into the diner and shook my hand.

He said, "I'm Christopher Goodman. And you're Hazel Turner."

I said, "What the hell?"

He said, "You've waitressed me here in the past. And I also used to see you, last year, around school, in a very stylish blue FFA jacket."

Had anyone else said these words, I would have taken it as sarcasm and punched him in his pretty nose. But this kid was being serious.

I had seen him a lot here lately. He usually came in early, carrying a trombone. He would sit at one of Mildred Penny's stations and order hash browns. Mildred would giggle and blush. Then Mr. Trombone would watch her while he thought she wasn't looking. But of course she always *knew* he was watching anyway.

"Mildred and I switched shifts today," I said. "She'll be here a little bit later."

"No problemo," said Mr. Trombone. "Could you just give her this for me?"

"A stamp?" I said, looking at what he now held out to me.

"It's an unused 1978 fifteen-cent postal stamp of an owl," said Mr. Trombone.

"Is it special?" I asked.

"Not in the least," said Mr. Trombone.

"I'll be sure she gets it," I said, taking it from him.

"Thanks a lot, Hazel," he said. And with a final handshake, Mr. Trombone and his big bell-bottoms scooted out the door.

When Mildred came into the diner later I said, "So, you collect stamps?" A blush came over her face, the color of a strawberry. She broke out in this goofy smile. I noticed for the first time how pretty she was. And for just an instant I almost wanted to *marry* Mildred Penny.

I'm not saying that we became best buddies, but we ended up having a few things in common. Our mothers drove us both crazy. We both had big dreams. Mildred dreamt of being the owner of a stamp collector's shop. And I dreamt of being Jim Fowler, the field guy on *Mutual of Omaha's Wild Kingdom*. Also, Mildred was way too pretty for a shy girl. And I was way too smart for a redneck.

Hazel Turner was my exact opposite. She was an Amazon warrior. I was a ninety-pound weakling. She castrated piglets. I played clarinet. I would have been less shocked if an orang-utan had been standing there asking me questions about stamp collecting.

But I was thrilled. I pulled a magazine from my bag and spread it out on the table that I was supposed to be clearing.

"Is that a magazine about stamps?" Hazel said.

"Yes," I said, "*The American Philatelist*. A philatelist is a stamp collector."

"And *you* are a philatelist?"

"Yes. I am." I sat a little straighter.

"Sounds suspiciously like fellatio to me," she said. "Do you suppose there's a magazine about fellatio called *The American Fellatio-ist*?"

"Uh," I said.

"Did you know," said Hazel with a wide grin, "that you look like a strawberry when you blush?"

"Uh, well, yes," I said. "I know it's kinda weird."

"No, not weird at all," said Hazel. "It's kinda cute, really. From now on I'll call you Strawberry."

"Uh," I said.

"I'm just yanking your chain, girl. Tell me all about stamps." I opened the magazine.

"I'm looking for George Washington, the Elder Statesman," I said.

"Come again?"

I pointed at a series of tiny photos and said, "It's a set of stamps. Famous portraits of George Washington, each from a different phase of his life. I only need one more to complete the set. It's called the Elder Statesman."

"Mm-hmm," said Hazel.

"Sorry. I know that probably sounds pathetic," I said, closing the magazine.

"Hell girl, I collect pig testicles in a mason jar. Who am *I* to judge? But I don't get all apologetic about it. *That's* what's pathetic. I never apologize for being me."

Without thinking I squeaked, "Sorry."

"There she goes again!" said Hazel. But then she smiled, and for an instant I saw friendship.

"Sorry," I said again.

"Enough with the sorry, girl. Now one last thing before we get back to work," she said, grinning again. "Who *is* that boy, Mr. Trombone, with the fancy pants? Is he your boyfriend?"

"Oh. No. We're friends. I guess. I don't know. He just knows that—that I collect stamps," I stammered. "He's nice like that . . . to everyone."

"I know he brought you a stamp," Hazel raised a suggestive eyebrow. "But is he going to *lick* it for you?"

"Uh," I said.

"You're turning into a strawberry again, so it must be true. Mr. Trombone must be licking your stamps."

"No. He. Is. Not. Licking. My. Stamps," I shouted in a whisper.

"Okay. Okay. Whatever you say . . . Strawberry!"

As a gift to the members of the marching band, the band booster club hosted a big picnic in a willow-shaded park on the bank of the New River. There was food, drink, horseshoes, and volleyball. Swimming and tubing. And, as always, there was basking on the chain of large rocks that reached out across the wide river. The largest of these rocks was, of course, the Jump. And that's where most of the band members ended up after they had eaten all the food.

The boosters had rented Squib and his ding-a-ling truck for a couple hours as part of the festivities. I had swapped a ride with him in return for an hour of my help. Squib was in rare form.

"Step right up! Step right up! *Fssst*. Boys and girls, young and old, brass and woodwinds," shouted Squib. "Today only: slightly odd and inferior off-brand ice cream, free, *fssst* compliments of your beloved band booster club and Kaplan's Ice Cream Van!"

After only thirty minutes of "Pop Goes the Weasel," the beloved band boosters told Squib he'd have to either turn off the music or leave.

Finally the picnic grounds emptied out as folks gradually migrated into the river and waded toward the Jump.

"Gimme *fssst* about fifteen minutes to close up the ding-a-ling, Doc. Then I'll be ready to hit the rock," said Squib.

"I tell you what, Squib," I said. "That water is calling my name. I'm going on ahead. By myself."

"Okay," said Squib. "You go ahead, *fssst* and I'll catch up."

"All right," I said.

47

"Remember," shouted Squib, "They open the dam upstream just before sunset! So we'd better take the safe way *fssst* when we come back!"

"I've got this, Squib," I said. "Jesus! Are you my mother?" It came out harsher than I intended. Squib didn't say anything back, which meant I had hurt his feelings ... again. I should have said I was sorry, but I was mad at him for acting so weird.

Instead I said, "I was hoping to have a moment or two alone." Which made me feel a lot worse than "I'm sorry" would have.

He said, "You want to go out to those rocks covered with people ... in order to have a moment alone?"

I felt like a jerk. And to feel like a jerk made me feel guilty. And to feel guilty made me feel even more angry with Squib for having made me feel these feelings in the first place.

So I walked away.

For weeks I had been wondering if Doc still liked me or if he just found me annoying. Well, that day at the river I felt the two possibilities collapse. And the end result was pretty clear. Even to me. After Doc yelled at me that day, I decided to stay put and not go to the Jump. Why go all that way just to be annoying, right?

So I put away the ice cream. Closed up the van.

And I stayed, like an idiot, and waited to give Doc a ride home.

Doc Chestnut • *The Sleepwalker*

I knew if he followed me that Squib would take the "safe way" to the Jump. He would wade carefully across the uneven shallows and then crabwalk on all fours, feetfirst with the current. To save time I went the dangerous way, starting downstream of the rocks where the water was deeper and faster. And I swam for it. By the time I reached the Jump, the crowd was rocking. The whole trombone section was at the center of the chaos, with Christopher Goodman as their ringleader. Their latest game was to take the word *ennui,* and pronounce it "yaawn-WHEEEE," pretending to yawn, then tightening their lips into an over-the-top smile.

"It means boring," yelled out Christopher Goodman. "But you *make* it exciting! It begins like a yawn. But it ends like fireworks!" He was wearing a pair of cutoff jeans. He was thin and evenly bronzed. I, on the other hand, wore a store-bought swimsuit that my mom had picked out. And my neck, chest, and arms were crosshatched with tan lines.

Everyone was laughing hysterically and having a good time. Then I spied Mildred Penny, and my heart lurched a little. She was smiling but sitting off by herself. She wasn't in a swimsuit, just shorts and a T-shirt. Her hair was dry, which meant she had come the safe way.

I took a breath and sucked in my stomach. And I made my approach.

"Is this rock taken?" I said.

"Oh, hey, Doc," she said. "No, go ahead."

"I see you took the safe way," I said.

"What do you mean?"

"I mean—I can see how dry your hair is. So you must have come the safe way."

"Yes, I guess so. Is that what you call it?"

"Yes. But that's cool. You know. It's. Uh. Safer." I felt like I was boring her. I was even boring my*self*.

Christopher Goodman did a goofy cannonball off the rock and shouted out, "Yaawwwn-WHEEEE!" all the way down. Pretty soon everyone started jumping off the rock.

"Yaawwwn-WHEEEE!" *Splash.*

"Yaawwwn-WHEEEE!" *Splash.*

"Yaawwwn-WHEEEE!" *Splash.*

I sat there with Mildred Penny. My armpits were sweating. More kids shouted. More kids jumped. *Splash. Splash. Splash.* The sun dropped behind the mountains that towered over the river. I realized, eventually, that we were alone. Just me and Mildred Penny. Sitting with only a couple feet between us.

"Are you going to jump?" I asked her.

"Oh, no," she said. "You go ahead, though."

I punched her arm. As if I was a nine-year-old. And I said, "What? Are you scared?" I meant to be playful. But it came out sounding pretty mean.

"I guess so," she said. "You go ahead. I'll take the safe way back."

At that moment Christopher Goodman climbed back onto the rock. Dripping. His body gleamed. He wore this really cool puka-shell necklace that was impossibly white against his impossibly brown chest. He shook out his hair. He had great hair.

"What's up, Doc?" Christopher Goodman said to me, smiling. "The dam is letting out soon. Jump in, and turn your yawn into fireworks!"

I didn't want to seem scared in front of Mildred (or in front of Christopher Goodman, for that matter). So I jumped up and feigned excitement. And leaped from the rock with a hearty "Yaawwwwn-WHEEE!" And a splash.

I swam downstream and quickly went about a hundred yards with the current to the stretch of beach where the New River Mailbox stood. The box's lid hung open, showing a jumble of paper scraps—notes left, no doubt, by the recent wave of band kids.

It dawned on me, only then, that I had just told Mildred Penny she was a boring scaredy-cat. Then I had stood up and left her there without even saying good-bye. And worst of all, I had left her there alone . . . with Christopher Goodman.

"Hello, Mildred Penny," Christopher Goodman said. "Did Hazel deliver your stamp at the diner?"

"Yes," I said. "Thank you."

"I know it wasn't exactly a special stamp," he said. "But to me that's what made it special."

"You wouldn't make a very good philatelist," I said.

"No," he said, "I probably wouldn't. I prefer my stamps out traveling the world. Not stuck in a book."

"My stamps are not stuck," I said. "They are just retired world travelers." I was surprised how cool I sounded.

He considered this a moment and then smiled. Then he sat down on the rock right next to me. Just inches away from me.

"Would you like to Yawn-Whee?" he said. And he gestured to the edge. Where I would not go. I shook my head.

"I don't really Yawn-Whee. I'm kinda chicken."

"That's cool," said Christopher. "But you can Yawn-Whee without jumping off a rock. Yawn-Whee is not just a verb. Yawn-Whee is a state of mind. Yawn-Whee is not *doing*; it is *being*."

He crossed his legs, closed his eyes, and chanted, "Yaaaaaaaaaaawn-WHEEEE!" Then he said, "Now you try it, Mildred Penny."

I crossed my legs. Pressed my palms together. I closed my eyes and I laughed.

"I can't do it!" I said. "I'm too embarrassed." I was trying not to hyperventilate.

"Do not be embarrassed, Mildred," he said. "Haven't you heard me making elephant farting noises on my trombone? Now *that's* embarrassing! And if you haven't noticed, everyone else has left. So who's going to hear, besides you and me?" And he was right. The rock was completely empty by then, except for the two of us.

"Okay," I said, laughing.

"It is just you and me," he said. "Now, let's try it together, on three. One. Two. Three!"

And we both let loose a "yaaaaaawn-WHEEEE!" Sitting side by side. On a rock. In the river. At sunset. Legs crossed. Our knees touching. His knee cold and wet from the river. My knee warm and dry from the sun.

Then he stood and said, "I knew you had it in you! Well done. Now we had better catch up to the others."

"I'm going back the safe, long, boring way," I said. It was a stupid response that came out too fast to stop. But Christopher wasn't even listening. For at that moment he had his back to me. He was facing downriver, looking out with his hands held up. The descending sun suddenly flared brightly through a notch in the mountain, throwing light and shadow across his body, defining the muscles of his back and his arms.

"What are you looking at?" I said to break the silence.

He turned to me, now dead serious, and said, "It's beautiful. So incredibly beautiful."

Then his face went goofy. "Good-bye for now, Mildred Penny," he said. Then he waved. And he jumped from the rock with a loud "yawwwwn-WHEEEEEEE!"

And a splash.

I stayed, like an idiot, waiting to give Doc a ride home.

Even as the other kids kept walking into the park and saying good-bye and driving away, I waited. As the sun went down I waited. I saw Christopher Goodman drive away in his orange car, playing "Bohemian Rhapsody" on the radio. And I waited. And finally he came.

And we drove home in the ding-a-ling truck. And we didn't even talk. Not even *I* talked. It was a long, long, long drive. I pulled up to his house on Palmer Drive.

And as he got out Doc said, "Sorry."

And I said, "Apology accepted. See you in the morning for LSD?"

And Doc said, "Okay, dude. I'll see you in the morning."

And I said, "Okay . . . *fssst* and don't call me dude!"

Suddenly I was alone at the Jump, and Christopher had been right—the scene before me *was* breathtaking. The clouds were purplish crimson. The light made of gold. Everything shimmered. For the first time I realized that the Jump was just one rock in a whole line of rocks that made up the steep walls of the gorge rising on either side. Light played on the water. Fish jumped into the air. From around the far bend, a heron flew along the river's face.

I could just make out the beach downriver. And the beat-up New River Mailbox. And a lone kid placing something in the box. The way he stood. The way he moved. Even from that distance I could tell it was Christopher Goodman. I made up my mind to read what he had written. So I left the Jump, going the long "safe" way, along the shallows upstream.

I was still giddy and light-headed from my encounter with Christopher. I could still feel where our knees had touched. I was daydreaming. Not paying attention. Didn't notice the water getting colder. I had somehow veered off into a deeper channel where the water reached my shoulders. My toes strained to keep contact with the river bottom.

Then I was under. And I was being pulled against a rock. My shoulder scraped across moss and tiny snail shells.

I flipped upside-down. I panicked. I swallowed water.

Caught my breath.

Back under. Backward.

Down. And up.

I hit my tailbone. I bit my tongue.

I tasted blood.

       Then I felt—

a hand

around my elbow.

On my wrist.

an arm   around my waist.

Pulling me from the water.

Hunger McCoy • *The Good Ol' Boy*
Mildred Penny • *The Stamp Collector*

Hunger

Damn, girl. Are you okay?

Mildred

I think so. I'm just shook up.

Hunger

No doubt. That was *some* dunkin'.

Mildred

How did you get to me?

Hunger

I was just fishin' off this rock
when you came splashing by.
First I thought you was playing.
Then I seen that you wasn't.
How's your mouth? You're bleeding.

Mildred

I bit my tongue. It hurts. A lot.
Thank you, so much. It's Hunter, right?

Hunger

No, it's Hunger. Like a stomach.

Mildred

Hunger? Really? I've heard Hazel call you that. I figured it was just one of her nicknames.

Hunger

No. It's really Hunger.
It was s'posed to be Hunter.
But there was a typo at the hospital.

Mildred

Oh.

Hunger

The *G* was s'posed to be a *T*.

Mildred

And nobody fixed it?

Hunger

Mom says she liked it.
And you're Mildred Penny.
You a sophomore?

Mildred

Actually, I'll be a junior.
I'm not sure what to say. . . .
You may have saved my life. That was—

Hunger

Naww, you would have got your footing.

I prob'bly just shortened your ride a bit.

Is that your green-and-white Pinto by the road?

Mildred

Yes. It's horrid I know.

Hunger

No, the Pinto is a great car,

aside from the occasional explosion.

Mildred

Well. My Pinto hasn't exploded yet.

Hunger

Hell, girl, it's got four wheels and runs.

And at least it's a Ford. I got run off the road

by a Chevy last week. I *hate* Chevys.

Mildred

I better get going, Hunger. Thanks

again.

Hunger

Hey listen, Mildred . . .

you mentioned Hazel?

I know you been working at the diner.

Mildred

Sure. We sometimes work the same
shift.

Hunger

So, she's been talkin' about me?

Mildred

She said you were friends. Why?

Hunger

Never mind. It don't matter.

Mildred

Thanks again, Hunger. Thanks so much.

Hunger

Okay, guess I'll see you when school starts!

Mildred

Sure.

Hunger

Or Deadwood Days. I'll have a booth set up.
A taxidermy booth: *Roadkill Resurrections*.

Mildred

Cute name. Yeah, I'll be there. I might help
Hazel with her family's petting zoo.

Hunger

No kidding? We used to say
Hazel had a way with the *live* critters.
And I had a way with the *dead* critters.
Hey, uh, Mildred. If you don't mind.
Next time you see Hazel?

Mildred

Yes?

Hunger

Be sure to tell 'er
Hunger McCoy says hey.

•5•

DEAD CAT DANCE

Two Weeks
Before
Deadwood Days

Leonard Pelf • *The Runaway*

It's Lance on the phone.
"Hey, Lenny. Meet me at the bend in Roanoke Street.
Tell the G's you're walkin' the little dog!
I want to look at the gun."

Last week, on a dare at the Army Surplus Store,
I smiled my smile at the counterman
while Lance stole a blue steel .38-caliber pistol.
We wrapped it in Mrs. G's Cling Wrap and buried it
near the curve of East Roanoke Street
where Lance lives with his grandma.
I've got six bullets hid in my sock drawer.
Along with a black ski mask.

"Plus, I got some Valium
from Grandma's cabinet," says Lance.

Lance is one year older'n me,
but about ten years dumber.
He's a reject. Maybe we both are.
But at least I got my looks.
And at least I got my smile.
Momma says my smile is a gift
'cause it puts folks at ease
and it won't let on what's inside me.
Momma said to smile at the clerk at the Quick Mart
while Momma stole Dr Peppers.

Momma said to smile if anyone came to the door
whenever Momma would knock,
to check if a house was empty or not.
Maybe when I get to Hollywood
I'll be Bo or Luke Duke
and get to screw Daisy off-camera.
Lance could be Cooter the mechanic.
Or a alien monster.
We saw *Alien* down at the Lyric Theatre.
Lance could play the alien monster baby
who crawls outta the dead man's chest.
All snot and blood and flesh.

But me, I got my smile.
For me, there'll be a bigger part to play.

Doc Chestnut • *The Sleepwalker*

That morning, the *Goldsburg News Messenger* had arrived late, which meant my deliveries weren't done till late. The last leg of my route took me through the parking lot of Gables Shopping Center, where I was surprised to see my mother's car parked in front of Mic-or-Mac Grocery. I recognized it from its front license plate.

I would best describe my mother's car as large, boring, and forgettable. It had four tires, and it was gold—maybe green. But it *did* have very memorable license plates that read *Y-E-S* (followed by three forgettable numbers).

No doubt, I thought, *My mother is doing some early-morning shopping.*

I figured I'd leave a paper with a special note for Mom. *I'll write, "Mom, What's Up? Doc,"* I thought. *That would be clever.*

Leaning my bike on its kickstand, I opened the driver's side door. Nobody locks car doors in Goldsboro, Virginia, especially during the summer.

I sat behind the wheel, and I had only written as far as, *Mom*—when my pen suddenly ran out of ink.

No problem, I thought, *Mom keeps pens in her glove box.*

I opened the glove box. *Hmmm,* I thought. *No pens. But there is a book called* The Jesus Factor. *Strange.*

And as I was rummaging through the glove box looking for another pen, a man stuck his head inside the window and asked, "Hey, kiddo, what're you doing in this car?"

So I replied with total confidence and a smile, "This is *my* car."

"*Your* car?" the man said. "Let me see your driver's license."

"No, I don't drive. I mean this is my *mom's* car. She's in the store."

The man looked smug, as if he had caught me in a lie. Obviously he thought I was a thief ripping off cars.

"Well let's go into the Mic-or-Mac and find your mom," the man said.

I was a sleepwalker. And sleepwalkers always do what grown-ups say. So I agreed, and we walked toward the store entrance, his hand on my elbow.

Only then, did it hit me: That wasn't my mother's large, boring car at all. The large boring car that I had been sitting in belonged to *this* guy following me through the Mic-or-Mac with his hand on my elbow.

The car's smell hadn't been right. The car also had a cassette deck. My mom's car had only an AM radio. Of *course* it hadn't been Mom's car.

I stopped and tried to explain that this was all a misunderstanding, but by then it was way too late.

While I dutifully waited, he phoned the police.

Daddy and I always listen to two things in the taxidermy shop: country music and a local police scanner. Daddy prefers Merle Haggard prison songs, which is why I can sing every one of 'em. Taxidermy, done right, takes a lot of patience, so the music helps to pass the time. The police scanner keeps Daddy informed about what all his drinking buddies on the Goldsburg Police Force are doing.

"I've drunk beer with ever' one of Goldsburg's finest," Daddy always said. "And they're always polite whenever they arrest me!"

My daddy taught me everything I know about taxidermy, which means I'm pretty traditional. A lot of folks these days will skin the critter and toss out the carcass. Then they'll just glue and stitch the skin onto a store-bought form. I like to skin my critters but keep the skull and a few of the bigger bones in order to have a framework to start with. Then I make my own form, like a road kill mannequin, out of wire and wood shavings.

I've helped Daddy prepare enough animals for mounting that I can tell you with certainty there is definitely more than one way to skin a cat. I won't go into all the specifics of the different ways, but I *will* tell you that my Daddy taught me every one of 'em.

But as I sat there with that poor dead white cat in front of me I wasn't concerned about how I was going to *skin* it. The question most on my mind was how was I going to pose it?

The day that Chevy ran us off the road, Christopher Goodman had said, "Make the dead cat dance." Back then I had taken the cat home and made some quick measurements. Then I had just stuck the poor mama cat in the freezer for later. But now here it was, all thawed out before me, and I couldn't get Goodman's idea out of my mind.

How do you make a dead cat dance? They don't got the same bones as humans. They aren't really built for it. It was hard as calculus to me.

But even as I was concentrating so hard on the cat question, and even with Merle Haggard singin' "Mama Tried" on the stereo, and even with Daddy singin' "Mama Tried" in a whole different key—I *still* couldn't help but overhear this one particular announcement as it came across the police scanner.

Officer Sharon Broom—robbery in progress—
Gables Shopping Center—parking lot—
Mic-or-Mac Grocery—
Suspect description: seventeen-year-old, white male.
Name: David Oscar Chestnut—
released to custody of—

"Hey," I said out loud to Daddy. "I *know* that kid. They're talkin' about that kid on the cross-country team. He plays the bass drum in the band. Everybody calls him Doc."

"That's correct. We are in front of the Mic-or-Mac. Thank you." My self-righteous accuser hung up the pay phone, his hand still on my elbow, and looked me in the eye.

"If I don't turn you in, kiddo," he said, "you'll never learn your lesson. Believe me, I have firsthand experience with you kids."

"It's just a misunderstanding," I said again. "I thought *your* car was *my* car. They look almost exactly alike. They have the same *Y-E-S* license plates."

Within five minutes a police car pulled up, lights flashing. Then out steps a lady cop, adjusting her hat, shifting her gun belt. And she saunters over like John Wayne and talks with Mr. Self-Righteous who explains how he'd caught me red-handed robbing his car.

After I explained *my* side of the story, the lady cop said, "Let's see if you have any knives on you or anything."

I thought she was joking, and I was actually laughing as she spun me against the police car and frisked me. I stopped laughing and began to feel something dark inside.

I felt frightened. Embarrassed. Outraged. Incensed. And betrayed. The lady cop sent out my name and address over the radio to confirm that I had no outstanding warrants for my arrest.

"You'll see," I said to the lady cop and Mr. Self-Righteous. "As soon as my folks drive up in the car, you'll see that I'm telling you the truth."

Not ten minutes later my mother pulled into the parking lot

driving her large, boring, forgettable car with the *Y-E-S* license plates.

Now, I thought, *Now we can clear this whole thing up. And Mr. Self-Righteous will see his mistake. And he'll laugh. And shake my hand. And pat me on the back. And say, "Oh I'm so terribly sorry."*

But Mr. Self-Righteous was already pulling away in his own nearly identical large, boring, forgettable car with *Y-E-S* license plates. And without stopping or even slowing down, he drove past my mother on his way out of the Mic-or-Mac parking lot.

And that was my first glimpse of the back end of his car and the bumper sticker that was prominently displayed there:

JESUS IS MY CO-PILOT

There is no way that Mr. Self-Righteous had not seen my mother's car. There is no way Mr. Self-Righteous did not know in that instant that I had been telling the truth the whole time. And yet he did not stop.

There would be no explanation. No restitution. No satisfaction.

There would be no laughing. No handshakes. No pats. And certainly no apologies.

Instead, I left the parking lot of Mic-Or-Mac full of hatred, humiliation, indignation, and

a deep,

deep,

deep desire

for revenge.

71

Leonard Pelf • *The Runaway*

Lance is talking about getting revenge
against the judge that wouldn't let me see my sister.

"You can shoot 'im down like a little dog," says Lance.
He just dug up the gun and now
he's pointing it at Scrabbles, who wags his little tail.
He pulls the trigger, and the hammer snaps.
"Stop it, you dumbass," I say.
"It ain't even loaded, Lenny," he says.

Lance covers the handgun in the plastic wrap.
And together we rebury it and take a Valium each.
Lance heads back to his grandma's.
I walk Scrabbles back to the trailer
'cause tonight's a twilight church service
and Mr. G said that if I went, I could drive.

I change into a dress-up-for-church shirt.
Then Mr. G shows me again how to work all the car's parts.
And it ain't exactly *Dukes of Hazzard,* but
it gets us where we're goin' — to a white church
just a little ways down Ellett Valley Road.

I know the road. Further down there's a few dark spots
with not too many houses around. Spots to take a girl.
Or drink beer. Or dump a deer carcass.
I sure as hell never been down this road for church!

Not until I started livin' with Mr. and Mrs. G.

The service is mostly singing,
with a good bit of hand-raising in between.
A little bit of altar call. A little speaking in tongues.
The only thing missing is snakes. I swear to God!
The entire congregation prays for my soul,
just as Lance's grandma's Valium is kicking in.
And they all praise Mr. and Mrs. G for being saints.
How they took me in. How they treat me like their own.

Then it's a long final prayer to the end.
The preacher talks. And talks. And talks.

Doc Chestnut • *The Sleepwalker*

The day after my run-in with Officer Sharon Broom, the cross-country team was running speed drills around the high school athletic field while the football team ran plays in the center. After practice Hunger and the Bronco Brothers gathered around me, like a herd of pachyderms encircling a peanut.

"If it ain't Doc Holliday," Hunger said, slapping me on the back. I tried to explain how it was all a misunderstanding, but there was still no denying the facts: Doc Chestnut had been thrown against a police car and checked for weapons. That was enough to make me the hero of the locker room. And the band room. And Mr. Fooz. And even the Jump.

With Hunger McCoy's help, myth quickly outpaced reality. By the end of the week it had gotten around that I was involved in an auto-theft ring. Furthermore, I had resisted arrest and was subdued at gunpoint by the county's first and only lady cop. I had been booked, fingerprinted, and mug-shotted. I had spent the night in jail. I was out on bail.

I had somehow sleepwalked my way to notoriety, and notoriety was nearly the same thing as popularity. I was still just vanilla underneath it all, but at least in those two weeks before Deadwood Days, I was vanilla . . . with sprinkles.

At some point I mentioned to Hunger how pissed off and resentful I still was. "Grown-ups are supposed to do the right thing," I said.

"I don't blame you for hating that lady cop," said Hunger. "Daddy says Officer Broom is meaner than any of the regular men cops. I s'pose she has to be, in order to deal with hardened criminals like Doc Chestnut!" Wayne, Wesley, and Eddie all chuckled.

"No, no," I said. "It's not the lady cop I'm talking about. I'm talking about the man who called the cops in the first place. I'm talking about Mr. Self-Righteous. I swear his car looked just like my mom's car. *Y-E-S* license plates. The same color. About the *only* difference was the Jesus bumper sticker."

"*What* did you say?" Hunger McCoy had suddenly stopped smiling.

"Mr. Self-Righteous," I told him. "That's the nickname I've given to the jerkoff who called the cops on me."

"No, not that," said Hunger. "What did you say about the Jesus bumper sticker?"

"His car looked exactly like my mother's car," I explained, "Except for a bumper sticker that said 'Jesus is my co-pilot.'"

"What kind of car does your mother drive?" I asked Doc Chestnut.

"I don't know," he said. "It's big and boring and I think it's green."

"No," I said, "I mean what *make* is it? You know. Does your mom happen to drive a Chevy?"

"I don't know," he said.

"How can you not know?" I said.

"I don't know," he said.

Squib (the ice cream truck kid) was able to tell us that Doc's mother drove a Chevy Impala. Not green, but gold. Just like the car that Doc had accidentally "robbed." And just like the car that drove Wayne off the road and made us kill the mother cat.

"Doc Holliday," I said as I put my arm around Chestnut's shoulders. "From now on, you and I are playing on the same team. From now on Mr. Self-Righteous is the opposition's quarterback. And from now on you and me are gonna do whatever we can to sack Mr. Self-Righteous and break his bones."

"How're you going to find the guy?" asked Wayne.

"Right," said Eddie. "You don't know where the guy lives."

"I don't know . . . *now*," I said. "But I heard the whole thing on the police scanner. And *that* means there's got to be a report written out somewhere."

"So?" said Wayne.

"So," I said, "The report is going to have Mr. Self-Righteous's name and address right on it."

"How will you get your hands on a police report?" said Doc.

76

"We won't need to," I said. "All I gotta do is ask my father to ask one of his cop buddies to read the name for us."

"And what happens after we *find* Mr. Self-Righteous?" asked Doc.

"We'll do what any self-respecting football team does when it's down by seven," I said, grinning. "We're going to go on the offensive. And we're going to even the score."

Leonard Pelf • *The Runaway*

The preacher prays.

My head bows.

My eyes close.

My skull feels

full of cotton.

I try to stay awake.

We give
        thanks.

We ask
        forgiveness.

We give and we ask.

But we never get.

We never get

nothing. But

a little

bit of

sleep ...

Doc Chestnut • *The Sleepwalker*

One night, when I was maybe ten years old, my parents woke to a loud knocking. Dad found me standing in our dark kitchen, holding a large, sharp knife. I appeared to be slicing an invisible carrot or an onion or some other dream vegetable — *whack, whack, whack* — against the cutting board.

When my father asked me what I was doing, as he tells it, I answered that I was making a sandwich for my little brother's lunch box. Odd, since I *had* no brother, big *or* little. According to my father, the knife flashed as it caught the moonlight through the window. The scene was disturbing enough that my parents took me to see our family physician, Dr. Fortini. (He had a crew cut and black hair on his knuckles.) Dr. Fortini called my condition somnambulism. He said I'd grow out of it.

And I *did* grow out of it, mostly. But there were times when I felt like maybe I had never fully made the transition between night and day. I never really knew what to say. I had the vague sensation that everything around me was staged by unseen playwrights. My house and my school were elaborate sets. The objects around me were props. The people were actors and extras.

When Hunger McCoy and the Bronco Brothers befriended me, I woke up just a little. Being talked about made me feel real. And the idea of plotting revenge against Mr. Self-Righteous made me feel dangerous, like I was not to be taken for granted. I had a true sense of purpose. And, at least for the moment, I was a little less boring.

•6•

MONKEY CHASES WEASEL

One Week
Before
Deadwood Days

Leonard Pelf • *The Runaway*

Another week goes by. Another Sunday service.
This one is in the morning like normal.
Mr. G lets me drive home, and he's "proud of my progress."
And I'm all smiles, but I've made up my mind:
I won't sit through another sermon — ever.
I take off my dress-up-for-church shirt
and change back into my AC/DC sleeveless tee.

Lance rides his bicycle over and knocks.
And before Mr. and Mrs. G can object, I'm out the door.
Me an' Lance take Scrabbles for a walk.
And we smoke Marlboros. And we talk.
"What you want to be, Lance?" I ask.
"I don't know. Maybe own a titty bar." He grins.
"They got titty bars in Hollywood?" I ask.
"Sure," he says. "I s'pose so."
"Can you drive a car?" I ask.
"Yeah," he says. "I guess."
Lance is dense as a locust post,
but he does have certain skills.

I ask Lance, "How much gas, you reckon, would it take
to drive all the way to Hollywood, California?"
"I reckon a lot," says Lance. "Maybe two whole tanks."

That's when we hear the music comin' from the ice cream truck.

> *All around the mulberry bush*
> *the monkey chased the weasel.*
> *The weasel thought t'was all in fun.*
> *POP! Goes the weasel.*

Normally on Sunday, Doc would have been riding in the ding-a-ling truck with me. But after his run-in with the law the week before, Doc had been spending more time with Hunger McCoy.

Doc's sudden anointment into the Bronco Brotherhood was bizarre to say the least. And I guess you could say that I took it kind of personally, since Hunger McCoy had called me Spastic Colon three hundred and eighty-five times all through elementary school (even though I do not, in any way, resemble a colon. Nor does Tourette syndrome have anything to do with the digestive process).

And although after eighth grade, Hunger McCoy had inexplicably and without warning *stopped* calling me Spastic Colon or picking on me in any way, I guess the sting still stung.

Because it was a Sunday, I stood to make a bundle. My customers were mostly post-sermon Protestants with no Catholic guilt or Jewish food restrictions. But as the poet Robert Burns said, "The best-laid plans of mice and men may often go awry." (By the way, Robert Burns also wrote the words to "Auld Lang Syne," which we sing on New Year's Eve. And don't you think it's odd that Burns would write one famous poem about looking *forward* to the new year and another famous poem about how all our future plans will probably *fail*?)

Leonard Pelf • *The Runaway*

All around the mulberry bush
the monkey chased the weasel.

"That's Kaplan's ice cream truck," Lance says.
"I recognize it from that monkey-chases-weasel song."

On hot summer afternoons just like this one
I used to walk my brother and sister to Kaplan's truck.
They must've figured I was the best big brother ever.
Their little fingers were sticky when they held my hand.
I remember a pretty teenage girl in a bikini
taking people's money and handing out ice cream.
Working the truck all by herself. Real distracted.
An open cash box in plain sight.

Before DSS split up my real family,
me and my little brother would distract the clerk
at the Quick Mart while Mom and my little sister
stole little stuff—fingernail polish or mouthwash.
I figured Lance and me could rob that ice cream girl blind
with all the kids out front keeping her busy.

"I got a plan," I say, and I hand the dog's leash to Lance.
Scrabbles starts yapping as I run inside the trailer
to my bedroom drawer. I feel the bullets
under my socks, but I push them aside.

And I grab the ski mask instead.

Back outside, I say, "Gas is near a dollar a gallon, Lance.
If we're gonna get away from this shithole town
we gotta think more like the Dukes o' Hazzard."

Squib Kaplan • *The Genius*

I parked the van near the graveyard on Roanoke Street. It may seem strange to sell ice cream near dead people, but there was a trailer park nearby, jam-packed full of little kids.

So I slid open the big side window. I propped up the awning. I put on my Kaplan's Ice Cream ding-a-ling cap. And with great ceremony, I flipped the switch to the electronic speaker that is always sure to elicit Pavlovian salivation in child and adult alike. I started the music.

"I am the *fssst* Pied Piper of Goldsburg Town. I have come to rid this fair hamlet of its vermin!" I shouted. "Suffer the little children to come unto me!"

And oh how the little children came running at a sprint. The adults brought up the rear, cursing under their breath, because they knew they were about to pay outrageous prices for inferior ice cream.

That's the way the money goes.
POP! Goes the weasel.

Leonard Pelf • *The Runaway*

We follow the ice cream truck music.
"You put on this ski mask," I tell Lance,
"And while the girl is distracted by all the kids,
you grab the cash drawer and run."

Clickety, clickety, clickety.

Scrabbles's toenails click on the pavement.
Lance giggles and flaps his arms.
We reach the graveyard. The music is loud.
A crowd has already surrounded the truck.
But instead of the usual bikini girl, today
there's this skinny boy with a goofy smile.
Every so often he jerks his arm
and spazzes and makes a funny sound.

Lance turns to me all excited.
He whispers, "Dude, look at that kid. This'll be easy.
I seen him before, in after-school math."
I walk slower. I'm getting cold feet.
But Lance elbows me. "Come on, Pelf,"
like it was his idea to begin with.
We walk by all those shouting little kids
and make like Bo and Luke around
to the back of the truck.

Squib Kaplan • *The Genius*

All around the mulberry bush
the monkey chased the weasel.

"Abandon all hope, ye who enter here!" I shouted, and the kids all giggled. "I am the way *fssst* to an ice cream city of wonder!"

You must admit there is something wonderfully incongruous about all these children clamoring for ice cream within view of the graveyard's gleaming tombstones. I made a mental note to one day write a poem about it.

But then I started thinking about pre-algebra, because I noticed a kid in the crowd who just seemed—somehow—wrong. And I remembered him from . . . from . . . from . . . the math lab! His name was . . . Luke? No. Lance. His name was Lance. Ha! Squib forgets *nothing*!

"Eat your ice cream, kids," I shouted. "It'll make you smart!"

Leonard Pelf • *The Runaway*

The monkey thought 'twas all in fun.

The big driver's side door is already open.
I look at Lance and whisper, "Here's the mask."

"I can't do it," says Lance. "That kid done seen me.
I told you, he knows me from school."

"That's what the mask is for," I say.

"I can't," says Lance. "I've got Scrabbles.
You do it, while I stand lookout."

"Lookout for what?" I say.

Lance hisses, "Go on, Pelf. You can *do* this!"

You can do this. You can do this.
I got so many people telling me all the things that I *can't* do —
But here's something that I *can* do.
I slip the ski mask over my head.
I suddenly feel real calm. "Bo Duke," I say.
Lance steps away, tugging at Scrabbles's leash.
Scrabbles strains against Lance and starts to whimper.
I hear Scrabbles growling behind me as I step up to the van

and slip through the driver's side door.

Squib Kaplan • *The Genius*

POP! Goes the weasel.

"POP! Goes the weasel," I sang out loud. I sang "POP! Goes the weasel" out loud no matter what I was saying or doing. I would just stop to sing it. Even if I was in the middle of a business transaction.

"That'll be five dollars and—*POP! Goes the weasel*—thirty-five cents, please."

"I'm sorry. We're all out of fudge bars, would you—*POP! Goes the weasel*—like a Choco-Crunch instead?"

It would help to pass the time. And to be honest, it felt kind of good to blurt out something on purpose for a change.

Leonard Pelf • *The Runaway*

Now I'm actually in the truck
and I can see the ice cream boy's back.
He's standing between me and the cash box.
And I'm moving really slow.

And just like I thought, the ice cream boy
is distracted with all them kids.

YIP! YIP-YIP-YIP! YIP-YIP-YIP-YIP!

Suddenly Scrabbles is in the truck with me!
And he's barkin' his head off!

Squib Kaplan • *The Genius*

I had just sold two Raspberry Royal Rocket Pops and a
Nut Butter Bash when, out of nowhere, this little dog
(specifically, it was a Chihuahua, which is a small, nervous creature initially bred by the Toltecs in ancient
Mexico as a lapdog) jumped into the van through
the driver's side door and started yapping so loudly I
jumped out of my skin.

Leonard Pelf • *The Runaway*

The ice cream boy jumps around.
He gets all nervous and yells,

"What're you doing? You can't be in here!"
He makes this strange noise, like a sneeze or a cough,
and he jerks his arm like he just got shocked.

Squib Kaplan • *The Genius*

And there's this guy in a black ski mask. And I'm startled, because I was not expecting to see a person wearing a black ski mask on a blazing hot day. (And the ski mask is knitted out of wool, and I think, *My God, he must be hot in that thing.*)

But instead I say, "What're you doing? *Fssst.* You can't be in here!" Which is sort of a stupid thing to say, but I'd never been robbed before. Plus, I can tell from this robber's eyes he's just a kid, not really a professional.

Leonard Pelf • *The Runaway*

The ice cream kid just stands there
so I push my hands into his chest.
I knock him onto the floor of the truck.
I grab the cash box and turn toward the door.

But my feet get tangled in Scrabbles's leash.

I trip and drop the metal box.

Coins clatter. Bills flutter all around.

Then I stumble over onto the driver's seat.

The keys are dangling in the ignition.

My mind is racing a hundred miles a second.

And it occurs to me that I could take the whole truck.

Drive away to Hollywood, selling ice cream along the way.

Squib Kaplan • *The Genius*

Then he shoves my chest and knocks me down, but
for whatever reason I still don't feel like I'm in danger.
Because this guy is just really not very scary. Then
the robber gets all tangled up in the Chihuahua. And
then (you won't believe *this*) he actually tries to start
the van. He obviously can't work a clutch. Plus, I had
placed chocks under the tires for safety. And, anyway,
what kind of a thief makes a getaway in an ice cream
truck playing "Pop Goes the Weasel"?

Leonard Pelf • *The Runaway*

My face sweats under the scratchy ski mask.
Hand on the keys. Foot on the gas pedal.
I turn the engine over. The truck lurches. Then stalls.
I hear a thud and I realize the ice cream boy
had stood up and just fell down again.
He's on the floor, holding his ankle.
He shouts, "What are you doing?"
By now the children outside are screaming.
I turn the key again. More gas.
And again the truck lurches and stalls.

"Aw, hell, it's got a clutch!" I say.
Then I turn to the ice cream boy.
"Why didn't you tell me it had a clutch?"

I grab Scrabbles, and I run like hell.

Squib Kaplan • *The Genius*

The van lurches, and I fall down a second time. And
there's a sharp pain in my ankle. I shout, "What are
you doing?" The kid in the ski mask yells at me. Then
he grabs the dog and runs. The whole "robbery" is over

in less than a minute ("Pop Goes the Weasel" had only
cycled through about one and a half times).

Leonard Pelf • *The Runaway*

I toss the ski mask in a trash can as I
cut through the graveyard, dodging headstones.
Hopping over the graves the best I can.
Scrabbles tucked under my arm.
Lance trailing his fat ass behind.
Eventually we make our way to the trailer park.
Lucky for us Mr. and Mrs. G ain't home.
The car keys are missing from the peg in the kitchen.
And there's a note on the fridge:

> *Shopping at the Mic-or-Mac*
> *Love you,*
> *Mommy G and Daddy G*

I had twisted my ankle, but the most frightening part of the whole event was the interrogation by the lady police officer. She had never seen Tourette syndrome before, and she treated me like I was an idiot. She didn't expect much from me, so I obliged and told her nothing. This was obviously the lady cop who had tried to arrest Doc. And the kid in the ski mask didn't get a dime. So, for once, I kept my answers short.

Officer Broom • *The Lady Cop*
Squib Kaplan • *The Genius*

Officer Broom

Why did you leave
the van door open?

> Squib
>
> Because the van felt like
> *fssst* an Easy-Bake Oven.

Officer Broom

Why did you have
an open tray full of change?

> Squib
>
> To make change?

Officer Broom

Why were you
working alone?

> Squib
>
> Because my Siamese twin
> was *fssst* removed in an operation.

Officer Broom

Why do you keep
flinching like that?

Why are you making
that noise?

Squib
It's called Tourette syndrome.

Officer Broom
Are you trying
to get funny with me?

Squib
Yes ma'am. *fssst*
I mean, no ma'am.

I didn't tell her about the kid's white skin (I saw his hands). Or the kid's five foot nine height (he stood a good two inches taller than me). His peach-fuzz mustache (it showed through the ski mask's mouth hole). The kid's shoes (white Adidas, blue stripes, probably size seven). Or his pants (Lee, boot cut, tear in right knee, pack of Marlboros peeking out of the right front pocket). Or his shirt (black, sleeveless, AC/DC). Or his accent (local, mountain). Or the Chihuahua (bred by the Toltecs). Or the ski mask (tossed in a nearby trash can). Or the kid named Lance (who was an accomplice).

This last detail was my own conjecture. I *inferred* the kid named Lance was an accomplice. He was the only other teenage boy there. And he was the only one who wasn't looking at the ice cream selection on the side of the van. He kept looking straight at me instead. And I figured it wasn't because I was wearing a bikini top. Because I wasn't.

And I knew this kid's name was Lance, 'cause like I said, *Squib forgets nothing*. And this kid had come by the after-school math clinic once during school. I never saw him before or after that, and I think he dropped out of school altogether. But I remember his name was Lance, and I remember the specific math problem. It was simple pre-algebra. He was trying to solve for x but couldn't make the equation balance.

Christopher Goodman was working with him that day, and I got called over to help out. I saw immediately that Lance and Christopher weren't following the proper order of operations. It was that simple. Lance looked pleased. I got the impression it was quite a big deal for him. Christopher laughed at himself for missing such an obvious solution. Christopher Goodman wasn't as good with numbers as he was with people.

Leonard Pelf • *The Runaway*

I try to mostly stay indoors the rest of the week,
after what happened at the ice cream truck.
But tomorrow is Deadwood Days
and there ain't no way I'm missing that!
I hear Mr. and Mrs. G pull up outside the trailer.
I help Mrs. G bring in the groceries and put 'em away.

"Thank you, Leonard," says Mrs. G. "I got you some pop.
It was on sale down at the Mic-or-Mac."
"Hey, kiddo," says Mr. G. "Did you get your chores done?"
"Every one of 'em," I say. And I ain't lyin'.
I watch Mr. G hang the car keys on the kitchen peg.

It's Friday night. *Dukes of Hazzard* comes on at 8:00 p.m.
But first Mr. and Mrs. G and me sit down
in front of the RCA
to eat Swanson TV dinners on TV trays.
I have a cold Dr Pepper from a can.
Mrs. G has sweet iced tea. Mr. G has milk.
Mr. G thanks Jesus for the shitty food,
then he walks over to the set
and flips the dial to Walter Cronkite on channel seven.
Maybe I could do Walter Cronkite's job.
    President Carter is down in the polls.
    Price of gas is up at the pumps.
You just sit at a desk and read stories.
    Gas stations charge a dollar per gallon.

Foster care separates brothers and sisters.

My steamed apples burn the roof of my mouth.

I want to say *FUCK* at the top of my lungs.

I want to put my boot through the RCA.

I want to get in Mr. G's ugly car and drive to Hollywood.

But I don't do none of that.

Finally Walter Cronkite says, "And that's the way it is . . ."

So I gather up the three empty tinfoil trays . . .

"Thank you, Leonard," says Mrs. G.

"Yes ma'am," I say back.

. . . and I toss 'em in the trash.

•7•

AS REAL AS A STAR

Deadwood Days
(Morning)

Hazel Turner • *The Farm Girl*

Long before sunrise on the Saturday of Deadwood Days, my parents and I arrived downtown and got to work. There were tarps to put down. Tents to put up. Straw and sawdust bedding to spread. Portable fencing to assemble. That was all for the petting zoo part. Next to that we had a big turnstile with four spars for the Pony-Go-Round. Daddy had designed the huge ark-shaped trailer to transport and stable every animal we had. And we had a lot!

The Noah's Ark Petting Zoo and Pony-Go-Round had been our family business since before I was even born. I had helped with the set up a thousand times or more.

We expected a big crowd, but nothing my folks and I couldn't handle on our own. Just in case, though, Daddy had agreed to hire on Mildred Penny as backup. It was actually my mother's idea. Mom had met Mildred at the diner and thought I needed a "normal" friend who looked petite and girly and wore a dress.

Truth be told, I didn't object. The College Inn Diner was closed for the festival. I was curious to see if Mildred knew which end of a shovel to use. And I wanted to see if Mildred would try to arrange the animals by size, color, species, or some other way.

Specifically, we had four Shetland ponies (for the Pony-Go-Round), two regular-size horses (to trot on the street), one Nubian goat, two sheep, two pygmy goats, one alpaca, four piglets, four chickens, two chinchillas, two rabbits, half a dozen ducks, and one lazy box turtle. I had raised a few of the animals myself. The piglets were my FFA project for the Virginia State Fair.

Skinny little Mildred was surprisingly tough. I think she even surprised herself. She assisted at the petting zoo, took tickets, handed out small bags of feed, filled water dishes, held up children to pet the alpaca, and swept up all the droppings into the manure barrel.

In keeping with the festival's western theme, Mildred came to work wearing a cute little calico *Little House on the Prairie* dress. I wore what I always wore—blue jeans, snakeskin boots, Western shirt, straw cowboy hat—and I fit right in.

It was my job to tend the Pony-Go-Round, just in case. Our Shetlands wouldn't have bucked if they'd been on fire, but little kids still find a hundred ways to fall off.

Doc Chestnut • *The Sleepwalker*

What's Up? Doc

I wrote it forty-five times on forty-five copies of the *Goldsburg News Messenger*. (Squib said it might get me more Christmas tips.) It was before sunrise on the morning of Deadwood Days. The stars were brilliant as I bicycled my route, papers rolled and rubber-banded in two wire baskets in the back. My headlight generator whirred against the rear tire. My mind was on the Deadwood Days road race later that morning. Squib would be by to take us downtown.

I thought, "Maybe today I'll be in the top ten." The bluster over my run-in with the cops had given me a new-born confidence. It was nothing compared to the bold swagger of Hunger McCoy and the Bronco Brothers, but it was something.

Squib had taken a week off from running to let his twisted ankle heal. We hadn't been hanging out at all. I was glad to see the ice cream truck parked in front of my house. It was like finding an old shoe you didn't know you were missing.

Squib jumped out of the van. And to show me how well his ankle had healed, he did his ridiculous Squib dance.

"I see you're still a weirdo," I said.

"Did you see the stars this morning?" he asked.

"No," I said. "I didn't notice."

Of course, I *had* seen the stars. They'd been magnificent. But I didn't want to encourage Squib to go off on one of his nonstop yaks.

We climbed into the ding-a-ling truck and began to chug away.

"Did you make a wish?" asked Squib.

I sighed. "No, Squib. I did not make a wish."

Then Squib began his talk about the stars.

Leonard Pelf • *The Runaway*

"Wishes don't do dishes," Mrs. G says
as I clear the table of Saturday breakfast.
"You can walk down to Deadwood Days later," Mr. G says,
"as long as you do your chores and keep your nose clean."

So I grab Scrabbles's leash and we walk to our alone spot:
a quiet place, with a lawn chair, by the trailer park Dumpster.
Mr. and Mrs. G think I'm taking Scrabbles for long walks
but mostly I'm just walking a few feet to the Dumpster.
Scrabbles has got no objection to me smoking.
Scrabbles has got no religion to ruin my day.

Mr. and Mrs. G—they ain't *that* bad, really.
They say they want to adopt me. That's nice of them.
But I already got a real family,
even though the lawyers are keeping us apart.
I'll take Scrabbles with me to Hollywood.
He might get homesick at first but he'll adjust.
I know what it's like having to live in a strange place.

Scrabbles curls in my lap
and he looks up at me with his big buggy eyes.
It's been a long time since I had anyone to take care of.
Then Scrabbles falls asleep on me
so I try to keep still as I smoke another Marlboro.

Smoke billowed from the back of Kaplan's Ice Cream Van as we pulled into the Gables Shopping Center. The starting line was located here in front of the Mic-or-Mac, site of my infamous "arrest."

The Deadwood Days road race was a fast one-mile-long course that started at Gables Shopping Center and followed Draper Road to a finish line, downtown, in the heart of the festival, among the vendor booths.

I was not the fastest distance runner at Goldsburg High School. Neither was I the slowest. I was what you'd call a middle-of-the-pack man. Squib, on the other hand, had talent to spare. He was a natural runner. But he never exerted himself, and he never won. Mostly he would hang back with me, in the middle of the pack.

And that morning's road race was no exception. A voice said, "On your marks . . . get set . . ." *POP!* A pistol sounded out. The pack of runners elbowed for position. All the while Squib stayed at my side. He never slowed his pace. He never quickened his pace. He never lost his breath. And he never stopped talking.

Squib Kaplan • *The Genius*

This morning the stars were undeniably awesome.

But of course, the brightest object in the sky was actually the planet Venus. Named after the Roman goddess of love and sex and fertility and who was raised in a clamshell. Venus is popular since, well, she *is* the goddess of sex. *Fssst* And she is always naked. Her breasts are usually about as shiny as the planet Venus itself, which is shiny and bright because it has a really cloudy atmosphere. But Venus is a planet. Venus isn't a star.

Doc Chestnut • *The Sleepwalker*

Somehow, Squib and I were sprinting at the front of the pack. But Squib kept talking. Only thirty seconds into the road race and Squib had already mentioned three of his main interests: sex, breasts, and outer space. Squib Kaplan could talk for miles about mathematics, or quantum mechanics, philosophy, tap dancing, or cats. He had something to say about everything. But his favorite topic was space.

Squib Kaplan • *The Genius*

Of course the stars only *appear* to be dim because they are a bazillion light years away. *Fssst* In fact some of the stars we see may no longer even exist. They are so far away that the light they once gave off is only reaching us now. Our puny human eyes can't tell which of those stars still exist and which *fssst* are just ghosts of what used to be.

Doc Chestnut • *The Sleepwalker*

We reached the half-mile point. I was running faster than I ever had in my life. My lungs felt as if they were being jabbed by invisible knitting needles. I didn't have the breath to tell Squib to shut up, even if I had wanted to. So he talked.

Squib Kaplan • *The Genius*

And how do we know that God isn't just a burned-out star Himself? Maybe God has already given us all the light He had. Maybe the only thing left of God is hand-me-down light waves. Like a rerun of *Lassie* or *I Love Lucy*. Maybe that's why war and death and acne all exist, because the stars we wish on today stopped existing yesterday. Maybe now it's just up to us.

Doc Chestnut • *The Sleepwalker*

Three quarters of a mile. We were still near the front, but I was nearly blind from oxygen deprivation. I heard only Squib's disjointed words. "God." "Stars." "Death." "Acne." My legs were cramping. My pace slowed. Squib stayed by my side. Runners passed us. A *lot* of runners. The finish line seemed a bazillion light years away. Squib was barely breathing hard.

Squib Kaplan • *The Genius*

Whether or not they still exist, the stars seem pretty real to me. I guess that's what faith is. *Fssst* I'm glad stars are up there in Heaven, even if they don't grant wishes. I think stars and God are both very real, but very far away. Look, here comes the finish line, Doc. I'll get us a couple waters. *Fssst* We'll have to rehydrate.

Squib put on a kick to cross the finish line, and he disappeared into the chute packed with exhausted runners. We had finished behind most runners our own age and a little bit ahead of the over-eighty class.

"Nice race, Doc Holliday!" It was Hunger McCoy, as if he'd been waiting for me. I was bent over, gasping. Trying to keep from losing consciousness. Or losing my breakfast.

"No. I—wasn't that—great," I said, stumbling slightly.

"I know," said Hunger. "I was just being polite."

"Hey listen, man," he continued, a wide, wide grin spreading slowly across his wide, wide face. His eyebrows were raised as if he'd just eaten the canary. "What are you doing tonight?"

"Just hanging—around Deadwood—Days," I said, still gasping.

"Well, change your plans," said Hunger. "I found out who Mr. Self-Righteous is."

Hunger leaned in close, dropping his voice to a sinister whisper. "And I know where he lives."

"Who's Mr. Self-Righteous?" asked Squib as he walked up holding two small paper cups full of water.

"Hey, Squib," said Hunger, "you're just in time. My grand plan for revenge involves you and your ice cream."

"What are you talking about?" said Squib. "And *fssst* you still haven't told me who Mr. Self-Righteous is."

Hunger explained how he and I had both experienced separate altercations with the horrible man "code-named Mr. Self-Righteous." Squib looked interested.

"I have a fondness for code names," Squib said.

"It took a while," Hunger said, "but one of my father's police officer buddies finally came up with a name and an address. I've got it right here on this slip o' paper. Mr. Self-Righteous is none other than Fletcher Grimshaw, who resides at 3016-F Eagle Street. Not even a ten-minute drive from where we are now."

"I see," said Squib, still holding the two cups of water. "And what's this plan for revenge?"

"I call it Operation Chevy Sundae," said Hunger. "We sneak over to this guy's house later tonight, and we lovingly place unwrapped ice cream bars all over it. Hot as it is, the ice cream will melt overnight. By Sunday morning, Mr. Self-Righteous will wake to find a Chevy sundae in his driveway. We can even leave a little cherry on top."

And then Hunger added as an afterthought, "Do you got any cherries?"

I finally found my voice again, "I don't think—"

Squib cut me off, "And where is all this *fssst* ice cream coming from?"

"That's where *you* come in, Kaplan," said Hunger. "Doc is your friend, ain't he? You get all that ice cream at a discount, right? How much could it possibly cost to cover a Chevy Impala?"

"Yes, Doc is my friend—" said Squib.

"Well, that settles it," said Hunger. "We can stick the ice cream in the Bronco, and Wayne will be our wheelman. I'll ride shotgun. You and Doc can ride in the back where Wesley and Eddie usually sit."

"You mean you want me to go *with* you guys?" said Squib, "And be an accomplice? A partner in crime?" I saw the slightest smile on Squib's face.

"It'll be fun," said Hunger. "And as far as I'm concerned, you'd be doing this whole town a big favor."

"I don't know, Hunger," I finally said. "I doubt Squib wants to get involved—"

"Why not," said Hunger. "Squib's your friend, ain't he?"

"Yeah," said Squib. "Why not? I *am* your friend, you know. If you want me to do it as a friend, all you have to do is ask. I'd at least consider it."

"What if the ice cream gets traced back to your uncle's business?" I asked Squib, looking for any possible way out of this.

"Even better," said Squib. "We'll just say the ice cream must've been stolen during the robbery last week. If anyone asks, I'll say I hadn't even noticed the missing *fssst* stock until just now."

"Are you serious?" I said.

"I suggest a combination of fudge bars and Caramel Delights," Squib went on, "for the best melt efficiency and maximum coverage. Melted Caramel Delights are *impossible* to clean up. And if we break them up into smaller pieces we'll increase both the melting speed and the affected surface area, all while minimizing the cost of *fssst* materials."

"Nice plan, Kaplan," said Hunger. "I like the way you think."

"Thanks, *McCoy*," said Squib. "So when do we do this?"

"Wait a minute. Hold on," I said. "I'm really not sure—"

"Tonight," said Hunger, ignoring me. "Most of the cops will be here at Deadwood Days. Wayne and I will bring the Bronco around to the street barricades where you've got the ice cream truck. We'll make the transfer when it starts getting dark."

A crowd in the street clapped and shouted as runners arrived, first a trickle, and then a mob. All of them looking like they were about to collapse and die. Running is not my cup of tea. Unless, of course, I'm running a horse.

From the petting zoo I could see Hunger McCoy talking to a couple of boys down by the finish line. I made a mental note to stop by and say hello to his mother.

A few minutes later, Mr. Trombone showed up, all smiles. He said, "Howdy, ma'am," to Penny, and tipped an invisible cowboy hat. And she said, "Howdy, Cowpoke," to him, even though he didn't look anything like a cowboy, in his bell-bottoms, puka shells, and John Lennon sunglasses.

He held out a set of keys to Mildred and said, in a John Wayne voice, "I happened to tie up my orange Maverick next to your green-and-white Pinto. And I noticed you left these in the ignition."

"Oh, my gosh," said Mildred. "I do that all the time! Oh, thank you so much!"

Then Mr. Trombone turned to me. "Howdy, ma'am."

I said, "Howdy yourself, greenhorn." He was full of questions. And he wanted to pet every critter we had. And he was particularly interested in my four piglets.

"What are those notches in their ears?" he asked, changing from the John Wayne thing to something very serious.

"The right ear tells you the litter number," I said. "The left ear identifies the individual pig."

"Does it hurt?" Goodman asked.

"They don't like it," I said.

"What happened to their tails?" Goodman asked.

I said, "Most pigs grown for meat have their tails clipped. It's called docking."

"Ouch," said Mr. Trombone. "That *must* hurt."

"But it helps 'em later on," I said. "Once the pigs are confined in a pen, they get stressed out and start biting each other's tails. And they don't have enough room to run away. With the short tails there's a lot less biting."

"Why not just give them enough room that they aren't stressed out? Or at least enough room to dodge the biters if they have to?" said Goodman. "Seems like that would be less work for you. And a lot more fun for the pig." Then he smiled. Mildred Penny looked at him like he was Gandhi or something.

"'Cause that's how it's done," I said. "That's standard FFA procedure!"

Mr. Trombone had kind of ticked me off. But truth be told, I had never really thought about it. The pain and squealing had always just seemed like a necessary evil. Since I was about six years old, I had been clipping teeth, docking tails, snipping testicles, and inoculating necks. And I could tell you a hundred reasons why. But I had never even considered that there might be another, kinder way to go about it.

Mildred Penny transferred a handful of feed to Goodman's open palm, and I could see her fingertips linger there longer than necessary.

I said, "Hey, Strawberry. Things are pretty dead right now. Why don't you take a break while you can, before the afternoon rush."

Mildred said, "What afternoon rush?"

"Mildred!" I barked at her and gave her a look. "Time to take a break. Y'all go walk around a little."

Mr. Trombone picked up on his cue.

"I'm going to head over to the main stage," said Goodman, "To record a couple bands. My tape deck is back at my car. We could check out some of the booths along the way."

"There you go," I told Mildred. "You can go help him push the fast-forward button or something. Bring me back a funnel cake."

And off they went. Mr. Trombone and little Miss Stamp Licker.

"Thank God they're gone," I said under my breath. Then I turned to consider the four little piglets with their docked tails and their notched ears

"Hmmm," I said. "Okay, Mr. Trombone. I'll look into that."

"Okay, men," said Hunger. "I'll see you after dark for Operation Chevy Sundae!" Then he swaggered back toward the Roadkill Resurrections booth, leaving Squib and me to stare at each other.

"What just happened, Squib?" I asked.

"It's called Operation Chevy Sundae," he said.

"I know," I said. "But why did you agree to it?"

"Because we're friends," said Squib.

By this time, most of the runners had dispersed and reassembled next to Dave's Dawgs to await the awards ceremony. Squib still held the two cups of water.

"Here," he said. "Drink this. You gotta stay hydrated."

"No thanks," I said. "I'm not thirsty."

"Why are you suddenly friends with Hunger McCoy?" asked Squib.

"I'm not," I said.

"It *looks* like you are."

"Well, I'm not," I said.

"Do you remember how Hunger McCoy called me Spastic Colon three hundred and eighty-five times between first grade and eighth grade?"

"But he stopped," I said.

"And now the two of you are best buddies?" said Squib.

"What business is it of yours who I'm friends with?" I said, trying to keep my voice down.

"You mean '*whom* I'm friends with,'" Squib corrected. "And you shouldn't end a sentence in a preposition."

"Shut up, Squib," I said. My voice was louder now.

"Sorry," said Squib. "*Fssst* Here *fssst* drink this." Once more, he held out the paper cup.

"No *thank* you, Squib," I said. "I. Am. Not. Thirsty."

He said again, "You have to stay hydrated." He kept pushing the cup at me.

"Jesus, Squib. I said no!" I was yelling now. "Can't you take a freakin' hint? You're not my mommy. And stop being such an incredibly spastic weirdo!"

It was all out of my mouth before I could stop it.

"Listen. Squib, I—" I tried to reel it back in.

"All right, *fssst* all right," said Squib, cutting me off. His voice was very calm now. He was trying to smile, but I could see tears forming. "No problem, Doc. But now that I think about it. You and Hunger better do the revenge thing without me. It's not really worth the risk, for me, statistically speaking. And I've got to get back to the ice cream *fssst* now."

"I'm sorry, Squib. I didn't mean—" I tried to apologize. Squib dumped out both waters then awkwardly looked left and right for a trash can to toss the empty cups in. He finally just walked away holding the cups in his hand.

"Wait a minute, Squib. Stop!" I said. But he didn't stop.

I watched him go. And we both got smaller and smaller and smaller as he silently walked away.

Mildred Penny • *The Stamp Collector*

As Christopher and I walked through the noisy commotion of Deadwood Days, I felt light-headed. If Christopher felt as giddy as me, he certainly didn't show it.

"I like Hazel," he said.

"Really?" I said.

"Yes, really," he laughed. "I think she's a straight shooter."

"She wants to be a large-animal veterinarian," I said. "She's going to apply to UC Davis in California."

"Excellent," said Christopher. "She'll do great. Those little pigs are lucky to have her."

I got a little tongue-tied. But Christopher always had something to say.

"I hate that there's a weight limit," he went on. "To ride the ponies. I wish I were a very tiny man, so I could ride a very tiny horse."

"You could always ride a normal-size horse," I said.

"I've never done it," he said. "But I'd like to someday. Have you?"

"No," I said. "Never."

"And what do *you* want to be, Mildred Penny?" Christopher asked. "Will you be a professional jelly-packet sorter one day?"

"No," I said. "But I could see myself owning a collectibles shop. For stamps and coins and maybe used books." I thought, *Was that a lame thing to say?*

"Ah, nice," he said. "And maybe records? You ought to sell record albums and cassettes and guitar strings. Everybody wants music."

"Hmmm. I never considered that. That's a good idea."

"I've got a thousand good ideas," he said. "I hate to choose. But life is short."

"What would you choose?" I asked. "If you had to choose, I mean."

"Right now, I would choose to go get the tape recorder out of my car. There's a band called Electric Woodshed playing pretty soon. I really want to capture the music."

As we made our way through the streets, Deadwood Days was now fully underway. The air was thick with fiddles. A banjo twanged. Bass notes thumped. A troupe of cloggers thundered on the stage.

"Ah! Can you feel that?" Christopher yelled. And he touched my arm.

"Yes!" I yelled back. "I feel it all over."

The music gradually softened as we passed the stage and snaked our way by candles, clothing, woven baskets, and drums. We stopped briefly in front of the McCoy family's taxidermy booth. A large sign read, CARCASS CREATIONS, FINE TAXIDERMY BY MARLIN MCCOY. A smaller sign read ROADKILL RESURREC-TIONS BY HUNGER MCCOY. I tried to introduce Christopher to Hunger, but they already knew each other.

"Ha, ha," Christopher laughed. "Hunger, you made the dead cat dance." And he pointed to an elegantly mounted white cat doing an expressive dance. The cat's eyes were closed as though it was lost in the music.

"Damn right, I made 'er dance," boomed Hunger McCoy. "I

call it *The Cat and the Fiddle*. But, you see, there ain't no fiddle. That's all in the imagination of the viewer, you see? It's deep."

We finally made it to Christopher's car. His orange Ford Maverick was parked right next to my ugly green-and-white Pinto.

"Thanks again," I said, "for grabbing my keys, before someone drove off with my car."

"I was pretty sure it was yours," said Christopher. "It is a rather, uh, distinctive vehicle. Plus there was clarinet music on the front seat. And an issue of *American Philatelist.*"

As he spoke he opened his trunk and pulled out a portable tape recorder with a handle. He shut the trunk and turned toward me.

There was this sudden awkward silence. I wasn't sure what to say next. I realized that it was really Christopher who had been doing most of the talking.

"Well," he said. "Electric Woodshed's going on in, like, five minutes."

"Okay," I said. "I better get back to the petting zoo."

"Oh," he said. "I guess I'll see you later?"

Did he mean, *I'd* like *to see you later* or did he just mean *See you later*? This was probably the moment when I was supposed to say *We close up the petting zoo tonight at nine o'clock, if you want to come by.* Or *I'm free later tonight if you want to share what you recorded.* Or *Come on up to my place, and I'll show you my stamp collection.* I said nothing.

And he said, "Would you like me to walk you back?"

And even though I *did* want that more than anything in the world at that moment, I said, "No, I'm fine. I need to get something out of my car." *Oh, my gosh,* I thought, *Why did I just say that?*

"Okay," he said. "I'll see you later, then."

I tried to say *yup,* like John Wayne, but instead I said, "Yeeep." Kind of like Minnie Mouse. I squeaked, "Yeeep."

And he walked off dangling the tape deck by its handle against his thigh. His elephant bells scraped the pavement as he glided away. Yes, he actually glided. He floated. As if he had no feet. Like he was walking on water.

"Yeeep?" I whispered under my breath. I smacked my palm against my forehead. One smack with every repetition: Yeeep—*smack*—Yeeep—*smack*—Yeeep—*smack*—Yeeep—*smack*!

Then I walked back to face Hazel.

Hazel Turner • *The Farm Girl*
Mildred Penny • *The Stamp Collector*

Hazel

How was your date with Mr. Trombone?

Did he show you his horn?

Mildred

Don't be gross, and it wasn't a date.

We were just hanging out . . . together.

Hazel

Are y'all gonna make babies?

Mildred

No, Hazel.

We barely just met each other.

Hazel

Is he gonna rearrange

your jelly packets?

Mildred

No, Hazel. We just walked around.

Hazel

Is he gonna lick your stamp?

Mildred

No, Hazel. We. Walked. Around!

Hazel

Lick it before you stick it.
That's what I always say.

Mildred

Oh, my gosh. I can't believe
what comes out of your mouth!

Hazel

I just like to watch you blush.
It's that Strawberry thing you do.

Mildred

Well you can just stop it.
You are a terrible, terrible person.

Hazel

I know. I know.
Here, I got you a present.

Mildred

Huh? Oh my gosh. Oh my gosh.
Oh my gosh!
A ten-cent George Washington
Elder Statesman!

Hazel

My God, Strawberry.

You have *got* to get out more.

Mildred

The cancellation mark says
Philadelphia.
Where did you get it?

Hazel

I found it at Grady's Antiques.

Mildred

Oh, then you paid way too much for it.

Hazel

No. I promise you. It was a steal.

Mildred

Well, you shouldn't have.
But thank you.
Thank you. Thank you. Thank you!
I can't wait to add it to my book when
I get home.

Hazel

That will be real exciting, I'm sure.

Mildred

Now I can start replacing them
with mint condition.

Hazel

What do you mean "replacing" them?

Mildred

The stamps with the cancellation
marks aren't worth as much as the
ones in mint condition.

Hazel

You mean an unused stamp
that hasn't been *anywhere*
is worth more than a stamp
that has traveled the world?

Mildred

Well. Yes. If you want
to say it that way.

Hazel

You mean if I'm a stamp,
I'm worth more if I've never been licked?
I'm glad I'm not a stamp.

Mildred

Oh my gosh, that's so gross.

Hazel

I bet Mr. Trombone wouldn't think it's gross.
Ha, ha. You're turning into a strawberry again!

Mildred

Stop.

Hazel

Hey, Mr. Trombone man!

Mildred

Stop it, Hazel!

Hazel

Hey, Mr. Trombone Rock-Jumping Petting-Zoo man!

Mildred

Please, stop!

Hazel

Will you please lick my
George Washington Elder Statesman?

Mildred

Stop. Stop. Stop! I can't breathe.

Hazel

Will you—

Mildred

Stop. Stop. Stop. Stop. Stop. Stop!

Hazel

Okay. I'll stop.

Mildred

You are a terrible, terrible person.

Hazel

Yes, I know.

Mildred

Thanks for the stamp. I love it.

Hazel

You're welcome.

•8•

CLICKETY, CLICKETY

Deadwood Days
(Afternoon)

Leonard Pelf • *The Runaway*

I help fold my laundry.
I make my bed.
I wash Mr. G's ugly car again.

Now I'm finally walking out the door
with Scrabbles on his leash.
"Promise me you won't meet
Lance downtown," says Mrs. G.
"I promise," I say. And technically it is true,
since I'm meeting him by the Dumpsters.
And Lance is there wearing an old green army jacket
and I say, "Why're you wearing that?
It's about ninety degrees. You must be burnin' up."

"I know it," says Lance. "But I got to hide the pistol."
And he pats his pocket.

"Why did you dig up the gun?" I said.

"Billy and Dean Harmon told me
they was gonna dig it up. To shoot at pop bottles."

"But I'm the one's got the bullets," I say.

"I *told* them it was no good without bullets," says Lance.
"But I figured I'd be safe and dig it up quick anyway."

"Just be sure you keep it out of sight," I say.

"No worries," says Lance. "This here is my gun pocket,
and this here is my Valium pocket. Listen. . . ."

Rattle, rattle. Rattle, rattle.

Scrabbles barks at the sound. Barks his head off.
As if Lance has a rattlesnake in his pocket.

Lance and I pop one Valium each.
We're on our way to Deadwood Days.

Doc Chestnut • *The Sleepwalker*

Rattles. Drums. Panpipes. And slide whistles. A makeshift musical cowboy band marched by. All around me revelers were reveling. But I stood there frozen in the heat. Squib had just walked away from me in silence. A silence worse than words.

"David Oscar Chestnut," I said to myself, "you are a jerk." Outside of Squib's own family, I was one of the few people he could rely on to see past his uncontrollable tics. And now, I had just called him spastic.

Here we go again! I thought.

I felt like a jerk. So I felt guilty. And that made me feel angry. Angry and tired. And tired of being angry. And tired of being the protector of Squib's tender feelings.

And besides, I had more pressing concerns—namely, Hunger's plan for revenge was spiraling out of control.

The McCoy family taxidermy tent was divided into two sections. Daddy's business, Carcass Creations, took up the big part.

Daddy's name is Marlin, like the fish. He's bigger and more doughy than me. Most folks think we look alike, except Daddy has a big beard, a beer gut, and three times the lung power. It was barely after noon, and there were already crushed beer cans at his feet.

Daddy's booth displayed mounted geese and ducks with wings spread in flight. Some large fish. An impressive bobcat. A series of wall-mounted deer heads. He also had deer-antler coat hooks, deer-hoof gun racks, turkey-foot bolo ties, turtle-shell sun-catchers, and an impressive pair of rocking chairs constructed completely of elk antlers.

In a smaller section of the tent I had hung a sign with letters made from a variety of small bones, tastefully arranged by my mother: ROADKILL RESURRECTIONS BY HUNGER MCCOY.

I started out simple. At first I just set the critter in a natural pose to give it a little dignity in death. You know, like a real resurrection. Like this chipmunk on a little log, here. Then I experimented with embellishments in keeping with the theme of roadkill. Like this here raccoon. See how his arms are outstretched and his eyes look all surprised? I call this one *Don't Follow the Light*.

Then Christopher Goodman had given me the idea to bring a little joy to the poor dead critters and make 'em dance. So I experimented on the white cat that Wayne ran over with the Bronco. See there? Mom says I really "captured the cat's humanity."

And keeping with my new dancing theme, look at this display of two little possums. It's kind of my hillbilly tribute to Edgar Degas; he's a famous painter. When it's done I'll call it *Dancers at the Bar,* like Degas's picture of two girls stretching at a dance barre in a ballet studio. But in *my* version I've got two possums in tutus leaning up against a liquor bar in a redneck honky-tonk!

It's a work in progress.

"It's a work in progress," Hunger was saying as he showed me his latest roadkill masterpiece.

"Are they holding little cans of PBR?" I asked.

"That is correct, sir," blasted Hunger's dad, who had come over to introduce himself.

"Name's Marlin McCoy," he said. And as he crushed my hand, I noticed he and Hunger were dressed in the same camo-print cargo pants and black T-shirt.

"Believe it or not, you can order them little cans from a catalog," said Marlin McCoy. "The toe shoes and tutus, of course, are handmade by Hunger's mother."

He gestured to a petite woman, attractive but frail, seated behind him in shade, her lap covered in a blanket, industriously sewing tiny satin ballet shoes.

"Mom," said Hunger, "this here is Doc Chestnut." Hunger's mother looked up from her sewing and smiled. Her face was ashen. She did not speak.

"Nice to meet you, Doc," boomed Marlin McCoy, butting in and slapping my back with an enormous hand. "So you're the dangerous criminal Officer Broom had to subdue!"

"Yes, sir," I said. "She really just searched me for weapons."

Then I pulled Hunger aside. "We've got to talk," I said. "Squib is out. We're going to have to terminate Operation Chevy Sundae." I was happy to be putting an end to the whole thing. And happy to be able to blame it on Squib.

"What?" said Hunger. "Hold on, now. Let's go have a talk."

He turned to his father. "I'll be back, Daddy. I've got to tend to some business."

"A'ight, son! I got this," said Marlin McCoy. "You boys go have fun."

Then he turned to me. "Good to make yer acquaintance, young Chestnut. Now don't go getting my innocent little Hunger into any trouble, okay, killer?" And he laughed a huge grizzly-bear laugh.

I laughed, too. To be honest, I was relieved that Operation Chevy Sundae had been derailed. As much anger as I harbored for Mr. Self-Righteous, I was still chickenshit at heart. When it came right down to it, I didn't have Hunger's courage. And I didn't have Squib's brain. The idea of retaliation, of striking back, was not in my sleepwalker code at all. It would require me to actually wake up. I found the thought terrifying.

Marlin McCoy turned and began to harangue another group of bystanders.

"Hold on, Doc," Hunger said. "Give me a minute to check in with the mama." So I waited and watched as Hunger McCoy, the six-foot-tall, 250-pound defensive lineman who held the official school record for number of sacks and the *un*official record for number of bones broken, leaned down and kissed his mother on the cheek.

Leonard Pelf • *The Runaway*

Clickety, clickety, clickety, clickety.

Scrabbles's little toenails go *clickety, clickety*
on the sidewalk on our way to Deadwood Days.

"Don't worry about it, Lenny," says Lance.
"Nobody's gonna see the gun. I promise."

I say, "Just don't accidentally shoot yourself."

"I know stuff, Lenny," says Lance. "I know about guns.
Besides. You're the one who's got all the bullets."

"Well, you're a regular Wild Bill Hickok, you are," I say.

"Hey," says Lance. "When I was in sixth grade
I was supposed to write a report on Wild Bill Hickok.
I never finished writing it, but I did some of the research part.
Wild Bill Hickok was a gunfighter, but he was also a sheriff."

"What?" I say. "Wild Bill Hickok was a cop? No way."

"That's what the book said," says Lance.
"He was half bad guy and half good guy.
He lived in a town called Deadwood, like Deadwood Days.
And he survived more gun battles than anybody. Hundreds."

"Then one day he was playing poker, minding his own business,
when somebody just walks right up and shoots him dead.
And they say he had aces and eights in his hand.
That's what they call 'the dead man's hand.'

"Ain't that funny, how a person can survive
so much for so long and then one day—Pop!—
and it's all over just like that."

Clickety, clickety, clickety, clickety.

"I guess we'll have to terminate the payback," Doc said.

"Terminate the payback?" I said. "No way." And I meant it. "We just have to come up with another plan. Wayne has already agreed to drive the Bronco. It's all set. We cannot allow Mr. Self-Righteous to get away without getting his due."

Doc said, "I'm not really all that mad anymore. Maybe we should just drop it."

"Doc," I said. "You can't allow people to dump on you. It's like Hazel says: 'If it ain't your horse, don't shovel the shit.'"

"What does that even mean?" said Doc. "And who is Hazel?"

"Hazel Turner. We used to be a thing. But now we're not," I said.

"You mean the petting zoo pony girl?" said Doc. "She's your girlfriend?"

"She *was* my girlfriend," I said. "But I had to call it quits. She was way too clingy. And I really can't commit to just one girl, you know."

Truth be told, I didn't really know *what* had happened with me 'n' Hazel. I had even helped her take the petting zoo to a couple birthday parties. I *thought* it was going okay. Then suddenly it wasn't. It was all happening at the same time Mom first got sick.

Of course I didn't say none of this to Doc Chestnut. "Let's just say I shoveled my share of petting zoo poop."

Just then I was struck by a brilliant idea.

"Poop!" I shouted to Doc. " Petting zoo poop!"

Doc just looked confused.

"Doc," I said. "I just got the best revengeful payback plan yet."

"Oh, God," said Doc. "Do I even want to know?"

"This is better than a whole mountain of melted ice cream," I said. "We'll call it . . . Operation Petting Zoo Poop! Come on, Chestnut, there's work to do."

"Where are we going?" said Doc.

"We have some shit to discuss," I called back to Doc, "with a girl I used to know."

Leonard Pelf • *The Runaway*

Clickety, clickety, clickety, clickety.

Me and Lance and Scrabbles finally arrive downtown.
"Deadwood Days is the best," says Lance.
A band of skinny guys is playin' rock 'n' roll
on a stage set up across from the Lyric Theatre.

We listen to some music. Check out all the booths.
Paintings. Pottery. Quilts. Lizards on sticks.
We check out the college girls. Gun belts on their hips.
Or dresses like the old pioneers used to wear.
Some girl sells kisses for a quarter.
I buy two and Lance buys four, but she's in college,
and you can tell she's ready for us to move on.

By now the Valiums are kicking in
and I'm beginning to relax a little bit,
even though Scrabbles's little toenails keep going
clickety, clickety, clickety like to drive me *crazy!*

We drink a couple beers from a keg in the back
of a black van in the Mr. Fooz parking lot.
A couple "cowboys" have a shootout
in the street with cap pistols.
Later, them same cowboys pass Lance and me a joint.
We're both suddenly higher than kites.

We stop over at this really lame petting zoo.
And Lance holds a rabbit and laughs his stoner head off.
And Scrabbles barks at a huge half-asleep llama.
And there's four little ponies all droopy
and sad and walking in a circle, goin' nowhere.
And I wish my little brother and sister could be with me
instead of just Lance and a little bug-eyed dog.
I could have helped them stay in the saddle.

Clickety, clickety, clickety, clickety.

Hazel Turner • *The Farm Girl*
Hunger McCoy • *The Good Ol' Boy*
Mildred Penny • *The Stamp Collector*
Doc Chestnut • *The Sleepwalker*

Hazel

Watch out, Mildred.

Here comes trouble.

Hunger

Hey, Hazel.

How you been?

Hazel

Fine as a frog's hair.

How you been, Hunger?

Hunger

I been good. You know me.

Mildred

Hey, Doc.

Doc

H-hey, Mildred

Mildred

Hey, Hunger.

Hunger

Hey, Mildred. Stayin' dry?

Mildred

Yes, Hunger.

Thanks to you.

Doc

What does *that* mean?

Mildred

Hunger just about
saved my life at
the river!

Doc

Really?

Hunger

Don't look so surprised, Chestnut.

Hazel

Mildred told me all about it, Hunger.
You're a knight in shining armor.

Hunger

Well, some think so.

Hazel

How's your mama?

Hunger

'Bout the same. See for yourself.
She's across the way. At the booth.

>
> Hazel
>
> Tell her I'll stop by. After things die down.
> I mean — well, you know what I mean.

Hunger

A'ight. Hey listen, Hazel.
Me 'n' Doc, here, got us a little project.
And we's wonderin' if we could
have your barrel o' manure.

>
> Hazel
>
> You don't say boo to me for six months,
> and now you want to borrow my manure?

Hunger

It is for a very good cause.

>
> Hazel
>
> What good cause?

Hunger

Payback for an asshole
who killed an innocent animal!

Hazel

Really? Are you shittin' me?

Hunger

Hand to God, Hazel.

Hazel

'Cause if you're shittin' me.
I'll add your balls to my mason jar.

Mildred

Hazel! Gross!

Hunger

If I'm lyin', I'm dyin'. Tell 'er Doc.

Doc

Yeah. It's true.

Hunger

This asshole forced Wayne off the road.
Which caused us to run over a cat.
A mother cat.

Mildred

Oh, no. Poor
thing.

Hazel

Mother cats take too many chances.
They're trying to feed their kittens.

Hunger

Ran us off the road and didn't even stop.
Come on, Hazel. I'll bring the barrel back empty.
It'll save you and your daddy
from having to dump it yourself.

Hazel

And who is your assistant, here?

Doc

Uh. I'm Doc Chestnut.

Hazel

The kid who got arrested by the lady cop?

Doc

Actually, she *searched* me
... for weapons.

Hazel

Oh, I bet she did.

Mildred

I heard about that,
Doc.

Doc

You did?

Hunger

Doc got arrested because this asshole
falsely accused him of grand theft auto.
The very *same* asshole who caused the death
of the innocent mother cat.

Hazel

If I *did* say yes, then
what's the plan for the poop?

Hunger

Me and Doc load the barrel into the Bronco.
We slip away after dark. Drive to this guy's house.
Then we make a deposit. On his car!
Then we all go to Mr. Fooz for pizza . . .
after me and Doc wash our hands.

Doc

Pizza?

Hazel

Okay, I'll give you the poop.

Hunger

You *will*?

Doc

You *will*?

Mildred

You *will*?

Hazel

On one condition.

Hunger

Anything. You name it.

Hazel

Mildred and I get to go *with* you.

Doc   Mildred

What?   **What?**

Hunger

It's a deal!

Hazel Turner

Why would I do it? I was happy. I was happy to have a little excitement. And happy to dish out some justice to an animal killer who seemed to have it coming. But mostly, I was happy to have my friend Hunger back. It felt good to be planning an adventure with him. We'd been friends since elementary school. We're both townies. Our families have lived here forever, not like the professors' kids. We're cut from the same cloth. So it felt good to be friends again, without the weird romantic expectations getting in the way.

Mildred Penny

Why would I do it? I was angry. I was feeling like a loser for being so awkward and tongue-tied around Christopher Goodman. I just wanted to go home to my stamp collection. But then Hazel Turner said, "Suit yourself, Strawberry. But I'm warning you. Unless you cut loose a little, you're going to wake up and find you're just another Shetland in the Pony-Go-Round." I got angry with Hazel at first. Then I got angry with myself. Why *did* I always shrink away from anything involving risk? No wonder I had nothing to say to Christopher Goodman. I never actually *did* anything.

Hunger McCoy

Why would I do it? I was sad. Not that I would ever *tell* anyone that. My mom had been sick for so long already, and every day it seemed to get worse. Daddy wouldn't talk about it. Not to me, anyway. And Mom would just pat my hand. She would say, "You know I love you." She said, "It's not your fault." She said, "There's no one to blame." She said, "There is nothing left to be done." I think that's why I started resurrecting roadkill. At least *that* was something I could *do*. And if there was no one to blame for Mom's cancer, at least there *was* someone to blame for the dead mother cat. Someone to be punished. And Mr. Self-Righteous was going to pay.

Doc Chestnut

Why would I do it? I wouldn't! I had made up my mind. There was no way in hell that I was going through with this! I had no idea how I would weasel out of it. But I was determined to find a way.

Leonard Pelf • *The Runaway*

"Any way you could buy us a couple beers, mister?"
I ask a loudmouthed drunk in a black shirt and camo pants.
"Sure thing, boys," he says. "This round's on me!"
We are at Dave's Dawgs with a case of the munchies.
They made us leave Scrabbles outside
tied to a pole or a bike or a tree or something.

The drunk says, "I saw y'all's little Chihuahua dog outside.
I mounted one o' them a long while back."

Lance says, "Ah, dude. You mounted a Chihuahua?"
And he starts laughing like a total stoner idiot.
Then I start to imagine this old guy screwing a Chihuahua,
with his PBR in one hand and his camo pants around his ankles.
And then, of course, I start laughing, too!

Then the old drunk man realizes why we're laughing,
and now the old drunk man starts laughing.
Big bushy beard. Loudest laugh I've ever heard.

"No," he says. "Not *that* kind of mounting.
I mean mounting of the taxidermy kind."
And he laughs some more and buys us two more beers.
And he keeps talking really loud, but I'm feeling fuzzy,
and I got no idea what the hell this guy is saying to me.

But he's reminding me of my own father in a funny way:

a big talker, and a big drinker, and — in the end — a big loser.
And I just want to get away from this guy as fast as I can.

"Come on, Lance," I say. "Let's get the hell outta here."
And we stumble out onto the street into the sunshine,
and it burns my eyes like I'm a damn zombie vampire.
I feel like I'm forgetting something. Something important.
Then . . . I . . . remember. . . .
"A car," I say. "Lance, we got to go find us a car."

"You gotta relax, Lenny," says Lance.
And he slips me two more Valium.

And I wash 'em down with the last gulp of beer.

•9•

OPERATION
PETTING ZOO POOP

Deadwood Days
(Evening)

Leonard Pelf • *The Runaway*

"We can ask someone for a ride," says Lance.
"Then we can pull the gun. Then kick the driver out.
Leave the driver far away, where there ain't no phone.
They won't even know the gun ain't loaded."

Eventually we end up at the Mr. Fooz parking lot,
and we split up, looking for cars with keys in the ignition.
Checking door handles here and there.

I ask one real big boy with a Ford Bronco for a ride.
But he's a fat redneck asshole and calls me a drunk.
And that makes me realize I must be pretty wasted.
I hear myself asking the fat redneck if his car is an automatic.
I hear myself tellin' the fat redneck to fuck off.
And I must be trying to pick a fight with the fat redneck
'cause suddenly Lance is there by my side again.
And Lance is tellin' me to shut up. Tellin' me what not to do.
 I turn around and give the redneck the finger.

"Fush you!" I say.

I called my folks from the pay phone in front of Carol Lee Donuts, but I got no answer. I was hoping they could pick me up. I figured no way am I getting a ride from Squib. Not after I've been such a royal jerk. If only my parents would pick me up, I could tell Hunger I'd been grounded or something. Truth was, my folks didn't expect me home until midnight.

One option, I thought, would be to apologize to Squib, so he'd let me hide from Hunger in the ice cream truck. But I was still mad at Squib for making me mad at myself.

So I made my way to the parking lot of Mr. Fooz to meet up with Hunger and Wayne. As I walked I tried to formulate some other excuse. But when I got there my attention was drawn to Hunger and some kid standing next to the Bronco. Wayne was not around.

The kid swayed some and then leaned on the Bronco's fender. He was skinny, wearing a sleeveless AC/DC T-shirt.

"Hey friend," he said. "Nice truck. Whaz she got under th' hood?" The skinny kid was staggering drunk, glassy-eyed, slurring his words. He obviously thought the truck belonged to Hunger, and Hunger didn't correct him.

"It's a 302 V-8," Hunger said, so cool, without even thinking.

"Is it an automatic?" the skinny boy asked.

"Hell, no," said Hunger. "Manual, the way God intended."

"Okay. Okay. Jus' curious, friend. You an' that fine car, I was wonderin' if you could give me and m' buddy a lift. Jus' a little wayz up—"

"Hell, no," Hunger said. "Do you see the word 'taxi' written on this truck?"

"Well, fuck you," the kid said, though it came out, "Well, *fush* you."

"I'll *fush* your drunk ass into the pavement," Hunger said. "Now get away from this truck before you puke on it."

Just then Wayne walked up, which is sort of like a refrigerator wearing a football jersey walking up. And he says, "Need any help, Hunger?"

"No thanks, Wayne," Hunger said. "Tiny Tim, here, was just leaving."

I was awed by the easy way Hunger handled himself. Maybe he wasn't a genius like Squib, but he made up for it through confidence alone. It was impressive to watch.

The skinny kid flipped Hunger the bird, then stumbled away. Then he joined a second kid. A little bigger. Just as drunk. I watched them jiggle the handles on a few cars. Locked. Locked. Locked. Then they jiggled the handle on Mildred Penny's ugly white-and-green car. Locked. Then the handle to Christopher Goodman's orange car. Locked.

"Hey, Hunger," I said. "I think those two boys are trying to rip off cars."

Wayne said, "Check out Chestnuts here. He gets busted for *not* ripping off cars, and now he's an expert!"

"No," I said. "I'm being serious. Those guys were jiggling handles."

Hunger said, "No time, Doc. You've got to stay focused here. The sun's going down. We've got poop to collect."

Leonard Pelf • *The Runaway*

"Lenny, those big dudes'll kick your ass," says Lance.
"And my ass, too. So just drop it.
I don't know how to drive a stick shift anyhow."

"What the hell?" I say. "You told me you knew how."

"No, I did not say that," says Lance.

"You sure as shit did!" I say.

"We have to find a driver a lot smaller than that guy," says
Lance.

"Shut up, Lance," I say. "Stop talking for just a second."
I keep walking by cars looking for keys. Looking for keys.
No more *clickety, clickety* from Scrabbles's toenails.
Finally I can hear myself think. And finally —

"Wait a minute," I say. "Where the hell is Scrabbles?"

"Oh shit," says Lance. He starts laughing.
"We left it tied up outside Dave's Dawgs!"

"It ain't funny, Lance," I say.

And we hurry back to where I think we left the dog.
But he's not there. I feel like I'm suffocating.

"Oh, shit—shit—shit—shit—shit!" I say.

"Calm down," says Lance. "Here man,
have another Valium."

With Wayne behind the wheel of the Bronco, Hunger riding shotgun, and me in the back, we wound through narrow alleys until we arrived at a small parking lot behind the Noah's Ark Petting Zoo.

About this time my sense of foreboding reached its peak. As much as I wanted Hunger McCoy to like me, it wasn't enough to overcome the fear that was percolating up through my throat. Somehow I had deluded myself that I could be a "somebody," but the price of being cool was just too high.

I had made up my mind. I had decided to chicken out. I didn't care if it made me the laughingstock of every kid in town. I was just about to jump out of the Bronco right then and there. I was about to declare that I'd have nothing more to do with this. But then—

"Hello, Doc!" It was Mildred Penny. Smiling at me and waving. Glad to see me. It was Mildred Penny. And I could tell, by the look on her face, that she was nervous. And she looked at me as if to say, "I'm so glad that you're doing this stupid thing too."

Here at last was something we could do together. A way that we could *be* together. By the time we had gotten the barrel of poop into the Bronco . . . by the time I had squeezed into the backseat next to Mildred Penny . . . by the time Mildred Penny looked me in the eye and laughed a nervous laugh . . . you couldn't have forced me out of that car with a stick of dynamite.

I was suddenly committed to the entire criminal adventure, lock, stock, and barrel of poop.

Slowly Wayne drove us past the barricades that blocked off the streets for Deadwood Days. Just inside the final set of barricades I could see Kaplan's Ice Cream Van parked, with its awning still out, a small crowd in line for a treat before closing. I winced a little remembering the hurt look on Squib's face when we last spoke.

Then Wayne suddenly swerved to dodge a traffic cone, and Mildred Penny had to brace herself with her hand on my knee.

"Sorry, Doc," she said.

"Not at all, Mildred," I said, trying to put a manly Bronco Brother swagger into my voice.

Mildred Penny was sandwiched between Hazel Turner and me on the back bench seat. Just in front of Mildred's knees was a thirty-gallon yellow plastic barrel. The barrel stood maybe three feet tall with "Noah's Ark Petting Zoo & Pony-Go-Round" stenciled onto the side. It was warm to the touch. It radiated heat. And even with the lid on tight, there was no masking the odor.

We left the noise and lights of Deadwood Days behind. Our way turned dark, punctuated by occasional street lamps. We rode on in silence and I noticed, for the first time, that Mildred and I weren't the only ones who were nervous. Wayne hadn't made a wise-ass remark since we had left downtown. Hunger kept checking and rechecking the address written on his slip of paper with a small flashlight. Even Hazel Turner had begun bouncing her knee up and down.

We drove past the graveyard on Roanoke Street, around a sharp curve, and—

"This is it right up here," whispered Hunger to Wayne. "3016

Eagle Street. Park the Bronco over there by the entrance. Now cut the engine and turn out the lights."

As it happened, 3016 Eagle Street was a trailer park. I had pictured Mr. Self-Righteous living in some big house in a rich neighborhood.

"We'll park here," said Hunger in a loud whisper to Hazel and Mildred. "Doc and I will carry the barrel on foot until we find the Chevy. We'll make less noise that way. You all stay with the car. Wayne, keep the motor off. But keep your hand on the keys. 'Cause once we make the dump, Doc and I will be running back faster'n Walter Payton. If you see any cars coming, honk the horn twice to warn us."

"Don't forget to bring back the barrel," hissed Hazel.

"Don't worry, Hazel," said Hunger. "Come on, Doc, let's go give 'im some shit." And he actually giggled a little.

And together Hunger and I slid the barrel out of the Bronco and held it, with some difficulty, between us. Shifting a bit to find a better hold, we both cradled the bottom with one arm, steadying the top with our opposite hand.

"H-hurry it up," Wayne said. He was turning a little gray.

"Let's go to the left," Hunger said. "I think this road is just a big circle 'round the park. Either way we go, we're bound to pass Lot F."

Then Hunger McCoy and I, holding a big yellow barrel of shit between us, slowly and awkwardly shuffled our way around the dark curve into the trailer park, looking for Lot F and a gold Chevy Impala with JESUS IS MY CO-PILOT on the bumper.

Doc Chestnut • *The Sleepwalker*
Hunger McCoy • *The Good Ol' Boy*

Doc

We should stop and put the lid on better.

> Hunger
>
> No time, Chestnut. Gotta keep moving.
>
> No tellin' if a car's gonna come by.

Doc

The smell is just—ho—ho—hold on!

The lid is sliding . . . off!

> *Clatter, clatter, clatter!*

> Hunger
>
> Ooops. Just leave it for now.
>
> We'll get it on the way back.
>
> Ohhhhh, Lord. The smell!

Doc

Hunger, the heat from the poop

is making my hands all sweaty.

I can't hold on to it much longer.

> Hunger
>
> You got to.

Doc

I can't. We got to put it down for a second
so I can . . . aaahhh!

> **Hunger**
>
> Don't let g—

Thunk! Slop! Slosh!

Doc	**Hunger**
Ahhhhhhggggh.	Ahhhhhhggggh.

Doc

It sloshed on my face.

> **Hunger**
>
> I think I got some in my mouth!

Doc

Oh my God, I am covered in alpaca poop!

> **Hunger**
>
> Sssshhhh! Stop laughing.

Doc

I can't help it. We are both
covered with alpaca poop!

Hunger

Shhh. Now you're making *me* laugh.

Doc

Stop! There it is. Lot F.

Hunger

That's the same Chevy, all right.
I got an idea.
I'm gonna check the handle.

Doc

What are you doing?
Are you crazy?

Hunger

He left his car door open!
I think the barrel is just small enough
we can dump it into the front seat!

Doc

You really *are* crazy.

Hunger

Absolutely. Now help me prop—this—up.
There.
Now, open the passenger side door.
You—pull the top of the barrel
while I—push it from the bottom.

Hunger and Doc had disappeared around the bend of the gravel road, leaving the rest of us just waiting. The only sound was a buzzing light above a nearby bank of mailboxes. A few yards away, a row of Dumpsters was illuminated by a street lamp. But otherwise the park was dark and quiet.

"So, Mildred," whispered Hazel. "Are you having even just a tiny bit of fun?"

"Yes," I said. "Maybe just a little." I was grinning. And blushing.

"And doesn't it feel good . . . to be bad?" she went on. "Once in a while?"

"Maybe once in a while," I said. And I smiled.

"So, Mildred," Hazel said again, "Mr. Trombone has been eating at the diner about four times a day."

"You're exaggerating," I said.

"You should invite him to join us for pizza after this." Hazel gave me an elbow. "He found your keys. He gave you a stamp. He doesn't come by the diner for the *food*."

"Sssssh!" Wayne was suddenly hissing from the front seat. "Did you hear that?"

"Hear what?" whispered Hazel.

Wayne's pained expression told us that, unlike me, he was *not* having fun being bad.

He said, "I thought I heard a car horn."

Hunger McCoy • *The Good Ol' Boy*
Doc Chestnut • *The Sleepwalker*

Hunger

Keep—pulling—Doc. Al—most. There!

Doc

Okay. Hunnnggfff. Hunngff. I got it.

Hunger

Now, let's shake it. That's it. Keep shaking.

Make sure it goes under the seats, too.

Doc

Oh, this is so disgusting!

He won't be able to drive

this nasty car for a month!

Hunger

Easy, Doc. You don't want the barrel

to press against the—

HONK!

Doc

Oh no. The horn! We gotta get out of here.

Hunger

Wait! We can't leave the barrel behind.
It'll give us away, and Hazel will kill us.

HONK!

Doc

Sorry! Here, just pull it out your way.

Hunger

Come around here and help me.
Slowly. Slowly. That's it.
Okay. That'll do it.

Doc

Hunger! Shhhhhhh.
The porch light just came on!

Hunger

Let's get out of here! Ha, ha, ha.
Go, go, go!

"I thought I heard a car horn," whispered Wayne.

"I didn't hear anything," said Hazel.

Wayne was uncharacteristically quiet. He tapped his fingers on the Bronco's steering wheel. He pulled a can of beer from under his seat and popped the top with a loud hiss.

"Wayne!" said Hazel. "You dump that dang beer out right now!"

"But I'm nervous," said Wayne.

"Well, toughen up, son," said Hazel, perturbed. "You're supposed to be the getaway driver. So dump out the beer. Mildred and I still have to tend to the animals tonight. And I'd like to arrive back in one piece, please."

"All right!" said Wayne. "Sheeesh."

"Get down, Wayne!" said Hazel, suddenly slouching into the backseat. "Oh, Jesus! It's the cops!"

We all instinctually hunkered down as a police cruiser slowly pulled into the entrance, turned to the right, and proceeded to circle its way around the trailer park.

"Quick, Wayne," said Hazel. "Honk the horn. You got to warn Hunger."

"I can't," said Wayne. "If I honk, the cop will just come back looking for *us!*"

"Then just drive the Bronco around to the left and pick them up," said Hazel. "If you go now you can get to them before the cop has time to make it all the way around the circle."

"No way," said Wayne. "I've got a whole twelve-pack of PBR

in the car. And my license is suspended. I can't risk it. We've gotta take off now."

"You mean you're going to just drive away and leave them?" I said.

"That's exactly what I'm going to do," said Wayne as he started the car.

"Wayne Wilson," said Hazel, breathing fire now. "You are a spineless, back-stabbing worm." And she hurriedly jumped out of the Bronco. "I'll go warn them myself."

"No you won't," I said, and I jumped out too. My feet crunched in the gravel. I wasn't sure if I had jumped out of the car in solidarity with Hazel or in fear of Wayne. But I heard myself say, "We'll do it together."

"That's the spirit, Strawberry," said Hazel.

"Y'all are on your own," said Wayne. "I'm outta here!" And he drove the Bronco out of the trailer park, spitting gravel as he went.

But he hadn't gotten more than fifty yards down the main road when a second police car pulled in front of him, lights flashing.

"Oh, no," I said.

"Let Wayne Wilson rot, Mildred," said Hazel. "If we run like hell, we might be able to get to Hunger and Doc in time!"

And we ran.

And as we ran, I wondered if inmates were allowed to collect stamps in prison.

"Come on, Doc," said Hunger, out of breath. "This is the Walter Payton part."

I didn't know who Walter Payton was, but I knew Hunger was telling me to run as fast as I could. So I ran. I was wide awake and running.

And I didn't think I could possibly be more frightened . . .

Until I saw Hazel and Mildred running toward us in the opposite direction.

"Cops!" said Hazel.

"Which way?" said Hunger. "Behind us or in front?"

"Both!" said Hazel. She stopped to pick up the plastic lid that we had dropped.

"What'll we do?" said Mildred.

"We're gonna have to cut across," said Hunger. "This way!" And he left the road, running between two trailers and disappearing through a stand of pine trees that circled the trailer park. We followed.

"Where are we going?" said Hazel.

"I'm not sure," said Hunger. "What happened to Wayne? Where's the Bronco?"

"He drove off with it," said Mildred. "But he just got pulled over by the police."

"If we get out of this alive, I'm gonna kill 'im!" said Hunger.

We passed through the line of pines and made our way down a steep slope toward the main road. We could see the flashing lights of the police car that had stopped Wayne. And we knew it was only a matter of time before the second police car finished its circuit around the trailer park. Only a matter of time before it turned our way.

Now out in the open, we'd be sitting ducks.

"If the cops stop us," said Hunger, "we'll just tell them we came out for a walk."

"And how will we explain why we smell like a barnyard latrine?" I asked.

Mildred added, "That big yellow barrel is sort of incriminating too."

Up the hill we could see the second police car now exiting the trailer park.

"Oh, gosh," said Mildred. "Should we run?"

"Maybe we should split up?" said Hunger.

"Oh, right," said Hazel. "So you and Doc will slip away like snakes and leave me and Mildred behind to get busted."

"Hey, Hazel," said Hunger. "It was *your* idea to come along, remember."

"Don't shift the blame, Hunger," said Hazel. "You're always looking for someone to blame. Well, this one's on you!"

I could see the second police car stopping to speak with the first one. I could see one officer pointing in our general direction. But Hunger and Hazel had suddenly become too absorbed to notice.

"Oh," said Hunger, "are we going to have this conversation right now, Hazel?"

"Yes, we are, Hunger," said Hazel. "Just once I'd like you to—"

"Quiet! Both of you!" said Mildred Penny, shouting more loudly than I knew she was capable of. "Listen!"

"Listen to what?" said Hazel.

"Keep listening," said Mildred. "There. Isn't that ... ?"

Hunger and Hazel stared at Mildred. We all looked at each other. A ways up the hill, I could just make out the second police officer returning to his car. But by now we could all hear the familiar tune. At first I thought I was hallucinating. I figured the adrenaline had been too much of a strain.

But as the sound grew louder and louder, it became more and more real.

"Hey, isn't that ... ?" said Hazel.

By then there was no mistaking it:

> All around the mulberry bush
> the monkey chased the weasel.
> The monkey thought 'twas all in fun.
> POP! Goes the weasel.

Before we could say another word or even take a breath, Kaplan's Ice Cream Van pulled up to us and lurched to a stop. In the next instant, Squib Kaplan lifted up the customer window with a clatter and said, "Don't just stand there gaping like a school of codfish. *Fssst* Get in!"

You probably wonder why I would rescue Doc Chestnut, especially when, just hours before, he had called me a spaz, and pretty much told me to get lost. And you may wonder why I would rescue Hunger McCoy, who called me Spastic Colon three hundred and eighty-five times between first and eighth grade.

I did it because Doc Chestnut was still my best friend. And although Hunger McCoy was *not* my best friend, he *was* my best friend's friend, which made Hunger McCoy *my* friend, according to the transitive property of friendship.

But the main reason I ended up being the wheelman for Operation Petting Zoo Poop was that I *really* liked the idea of being a *wheelman* in an *operation*. And I don't know if Mr. Self-Righteous really deserved what he got, but he had done my best friend wrong. And that was good enough for me.

A penny for a spool of thread,
A penny for a needle—
That's the way the money goes...

By the time the second police car descended the hill, Hazel, Mildred, Hunger, and I were all crouched inside Squib's van, well out of sight, behind the ice cream freezers. I still held on to the yellow bucket, trying to keep it (and its smell) an arm's length away.

"Everybody *fssst* stay down and don't move," said Squib out of the corner of his mouth. "We made it by the first policeman. Now we're about to drive by the other cop at the entrance to the trailer park."

"Tell us what you see," whispered Hunger.

"I see flashing lights. I see the Bronco with the door open and a twelve-pack of beer on the hood. And I see Officer Broom, the lady cop."

"What's she doing?" I asked.

"She seems to have Wayne Wilson up against the police car *fssst* checking him for weapons!" said Squib.

"Ha, ha, ha!" says Hazel. "Serves him right."

"Some friend *that* guy turned out to be," said Hunger.

"Okay," said Squib, looking behind us in the van's side mirror. "No one seems to be following us. I think we've successfully run the gauntlet."

"And why are you leaving the music on?" I whispered.

"I'm triggering a Pavlovian sense of calm in whatever

law-enforcement officials might be tempted to pull me over," said Squib. "Since ice-cream-truck jingles are associated with innocence, it will cloak whatever atmospheric vibrations of guilt might be emanating from inside the van."

"The only thing emanating from inside this van," said Hazel, "Is the stink coming off the two of *you*! What did you do, dump the barrel on yourselves?"

"Well, sort of," said Hunger.

"Just get us to the nearest hose," I said.

"I've got just the place," said Squib.

"How did you know where to find us, anyway?" I asked.

"That was easy," said Squib. "Hunger read the name and address to us this afternoon: Mr. Fletcher Grimshaw, 3016-F Eagle Street. How many times do I have to tell you, Doc? Squib forgets *nothing*!"

"Three cheers for Squib's huge brain," said Hunger. And we all cheered.

•10•

THE BEST-LAID PLANS

**Deadwood Days
(Late Night)**

Leonard Pelf • *The Runaway*

I've been searching
         for an hour.
I've been looking
        under cars.
               Listening for the
               clickety, clickety
               of little claws.
Down alleys.   Retracing steps . . .

past the funnel cakes and snow cones
past the candles
        and quilts
        and kettle corn.
               Listening for the
               clickety, clickety
               of little claws.
Backtracking past the rock stars
and cloggers and pot-smoking gunslingers.

    And voices announcing the end of Deadwood Days.

        By the tree outside Dave's Dawgs
          and a leash
           wound tight,
             so tight,
         around the trunk
       of the tree outside Dave's Dawgs

And the little red leash . . .

   chew-chew-chewed . . .

      all the way through.

The little red leash left frayed
my brother left . . . my sister left . . .
my brother and sister left afraid

Looking for the dog.
That the drunk man
once mounted. Haw. Haw.

     Listening for the
     clickety, clickety
     of little claws.

Sitting on the floor of the van, between the ice cream coolers, we talked and joked and laughed. Hunger and I relived our side of the evening's adventure. Then Hazel and Mildred relived their side. Then our two stories collided and ended in yet another cheer for Squib Kaplan, who had saved the day. We were all manic with adrenaline and relief at not being caught.

Mildred had moved to sit directly across from me, and as the stories went 'round our eyes would meet. And each look was accompanied by a genuine smile. An easy, comfortable smile that said, *We share history, you and I.*

I hadn't shared with anyone, not even Squib, the way I felt about Mildred Penny. Had I *declared* my feelings about her, I would have been expected to *act* on my feelings. Now, I was beginning to think maybe there really was the sliver of a chance. Between the evening's alternating doses of mortal fear and romantic attraction, I was about as wide awake as a sleepwalker could get.

Finally Squib turned off "Pop Goes the Weasel," as he steered the ice cream truck off Country Club Drive into a gated community.

"I'm stopping by my house," said Squib. "We've got a hose and some clothes you can borrow. My parents are going to be gone until late."

Squib pulled the van up his long paved driveway lined with boxwoods. He eventually parked along the side of his family's huge home, at his own private entrance, off of a tiny unused basketball court.

Squib had no curfews. He came and went as he pleased. And his big sister had moved away, leaving him with his own apartment downstairs.

Squib leaped from the truck and began singing "We Are the Champions." And he began to do his Squib dance, flailing his arms and legs like a total idiot.

I found it impossible not to laugh. Squib danced on, back and forth. And I knew if I didn't laugh, I would very likely die. So I laughed. And I laughed. Choking for air. For the first time in my life I felt fully awake, and it was surely going to kill me.

Squib sprayed out the ice cream truck with a hose. Then he sprayed out the yellow plastic barrel and lid. Then he sprayed Hunger and me both, fully clothed. Then Hazel grabbed the hose and tried to spray Mildred, but Mildred ran behind the ding-a-ling truck, shrieking.

The August air was hot and humid. The water felt cool.

Squib placed our wet things in the clothes dryer. And we waited, me and Hunger both wrapped in warm bathrobes. And we sat on the Kaplans' deck, eating ice cream sandwiches from the truck. Squib brought out an old guitar his sister had left behind. And Hunger played and sang a medley of Merle Haggard prison songs. And, I'll be damned if Hunger McCoy didn't have the most beautiful and plaintive voice. And Mildred Penny. Looking my way from time to time with those quiet green eyes.

Within the hour we were back downtown. Squib parked the ice cream truck in a vendor lot. The main stage was empty. The crowds in the streets were beginning to thin. People moved toward their cars or moved indoors in hopes of making the fun last longer.

"Come on," said Squib. "If we keep ahead of these people we can get a good table at Mr. Fooz."

"First Mildred and me have to tend to the animals and take back the manure barrel," said Hazel.

"And I've gotta help my parents pack up the truck and get back home," said Hunger. "Why don't Squib and Chestnut go stake us out a table. We'll all meet up there quick as we can."

"Excellent," said Squib. "Doc, that'll give us time to play Space Invaders."

"Oh I'm sorry to miss *that,*" said Hazel, rolling her eyes.

As the girls were leaving, I caught Mildred's eye and added, "See you at Mr. Fooz, Mildred."

And she said, "Okay, Doc."

Mildred and Doc, I said to myself. The two names sort of danced in the air as I watched Mildred Penny walk away, the hem of her pioneer dress swishing against the back of her calves.

Hunger McCoy • *The Good Ol' Boy*

After the girls walked away, I told Squib and Doc, "I'll see if Daddy can find out what sort of trouble Wayne's in. I don't think he'll rat on us, but to tell you the truth, I don't really know. Wayne didn't turn out to be the friend I thought he was."

I started to leave, but Squib said, "Hey, Hunger, that reminds me. I've always wondered something."

"What's that, Squib?" I said.

"Why did you stop picking on me?" Squib asked.

"Do what?" I said, confused.

"You know. You used to taunt me endlessly. Remember? Spastic Colon and all that? In fact you called me Spastic Colon three hundred and eighty-five times. Then one day you just stopped. It was noticeably abrupt. What happened?"

Doc Chestnut started shifting his feet like he was all embarrassed by Squib putting such a thoughtful question to a dumb redneck like me.

But the answer was easy.

"When I was a kid," I said. "I didn't even know what a colon was. Then my mom got colon cancer. Spastic Colon didn't seem funny no more."

"I'm sorry," said Squib.

"It's okay," answered Hunger. "It's going to be whatever it is, I guess."

By the time I made it to the taxidermy booth, Daddy had already rolled down the sides of our tent, and he was placing the last of our stock into the bed of the pickup. It was too risky to leave everything overnight. Mom was wrapped in a quilt, fast asleep in the cab up front.

In the very center of the truck bed, among the deer heads and antler racks, stood the white mother cat. Still frozen mid-dance.

I had sold only two pieces: One, titled *Left Paw Yellow,* depicted three resurrected chipmunks playing a game of Twister. The other one, two resurrected rabbits with little machine guns, I called *Bunny and Clyde.*

But the dancing white cat was not for sale. It was my best effort yet. I had captured something. I had drawn a little bit of life from her broken body.

And yet it still wasn't enough. The mother cat still couldn't breathe or tend her kittens. Her body rigid and cold. As I helped my father tie down a rope, I felt more restless than ever. The success of Operation Petting Zoo Poop had felt good at first. But the feeling was short-lived, and it only went so deep.

I sat behind the wheel of Daddy's pickup. Daddy, who had lost his license, sat shotgun. And Mom sat between us, sleeping with her head on Daddy's shoulder.

"Got a lot of compliments today on your handiwork, son," Daddy said.

"Yep," I said. "I'm learnin'. Stuffin' don't come as easy to me as singin'."

"You haven't picked your guitar in a while," Daddy said.

"I picked a little bit just tonight," I said. "Over at Squib Kaplan's."

"Oh, you did?" Daddy said. "I'm glad to hear it, son."

"I don't know, Daddy," I said. "Seems like everything that used to feel good just feels bad now."

"I know, son," said Daddy. The truck's headlights lit up the road ahead. The radio was only AM, and it was broke anyway. But after all the noise of Deadwood Days, the silence felt good.

Over the low growl of the truck's motor I could hear Mom's raspy breath. In a soft voice, like a lullaby, I sang a verse of "Mama Tried" by Merle Haggard. But the tune trailed off to nothing. And after a while, somewhere in the dark. The sound of my father sobbing.

Hazel Turner • *The Farm Girl*

During Deadwood Days my folks and I would spend the night in a camper to be near our animals. Mildred and I eased past the camper to the back of the Noah's Ark animal trailer, where I replaced the yellow manure barrel. Since I was in charge of the poop, I was pretty sure no one else would even notice that the barrel had been hosed clean.

My father had already put up and fed the animals. Hazel and I checked in with my four piglets bedded down for the night in a small crate.

But as soon as they saw my face, they became agitated. I could tell they wanted out. "Sometimes the pigs don't travel so well," I told Mildred. "They're just as smart as most dogs. And they are sensitive."

"Oh, no, look," said Mildred. "This little fellow's tail is bleeding."

And so it was. I put some antibiotic ointment on the wound, and I thought about what Christopher Goodman had said earlier in the day. *Why not just give them enough room?*

"You know what, Mildred?" I said. "I think I may have come up with a new project for FFA."

"What's that?" said Mildred.

"Pain-free piglets!" I said. "Thanks to Mr. Trombone."

"Come on, Doc," said Squib. "We've gotta get a table before they're all gone." As we made our way to Mr. Fooz, Deadwood Days was transforming. The sky was dark and starless. The streetlights cast phantom shadows. The vendor booths were shut down. Families with small children had gone home to bed. Crowds on the street were decreasing in number, but increasing in volume. Beer was available everywhere. Indoors in bars. Outdoors in ice coolers. A man in a van filled cups from a keg — fifty cents, no questions asked.

A group of tipsy "cowboys" rigged a string of flashlights to a weather balloon and sent it up into the sky to much applause. From time to time we smelled the earthy sting of marijuana smoke.

Squib and I abstained from the alcohol and weed. It wasn't really our thing. Plus we were training for cross-country in the fall; to be seen drinking meant automatic suspension from the team. Besides, I was already drunk on adrenaline from our night of crime and high on hope over my growing friendship with Mildred Penny. So many possibilities.

The sign above the entrance to Mr. Fooz had been covered with a banner that read THE ACES AND EIGHTS SALOON. We were glad to get out of the August heat. Glad to slip into the air-conditioned restaurant. And glad to have a chance to play the new Space Invaders game that, so far, we'd only heard about.

Mr. Fooz was loud and crowded. All tables were taken, so we put our names on a wait list for a booth — maybe a snug fit for all five of us, but after the events of the evening I figured we were friends enough to squeeze in. I imagined sitting next to Mildred close enough that our legs touched, the way they had touched on the floor of the ice cream van. No big deal. Just a leg touching a leg.

While we waited, we scanned the room for the Space Invaders machine, and we found it stationed in the far corner. And taking his turn, at that very moment, was none other than Christopher Goodman, flanked by his two friends, Tony and Mike.

Thump... Thump... Thump... Thump.

Christopher Goodman destroyed an advancing rank of aliens.

Thump. Thump. Thump. Thump.

Lights flashed. The score soared. The next rank of aliens marched double time.

ThumpThumpThumpThump.

The music quickened. Bells of nearby pinball machines *kachinged*. An explosion. *GAME OVER!* A groan of disappointment. Then *HIGH SCORE!* And everyone around him cheered.

There was a line, four or five deep, waiting for a chance to play. Tony and Mike stepped up and set the machine for two players. Christopher Goodman stepped away. He saw me. And he smiled.

"What's up, Doc?" he said. And then, "Hey, Squib." He seemed genuinely glad to see us.

"How's the game?" asked Squib.

"Fantastic," said Christopher Goodman. "But I'm out of quarters, and I've had my fill of killing aliens for a while. Besides that, I've got to get out of this air-conditioning before I freeze to death. I'd much rather be basking on a rock at the river." Despite the heat outside, Goodman was wearing a button-up long-sleeved shirt with a wide collar.

"I'll see you at marching band practice on Monday!" he said.

"Absolutely," said Squib.

"See you Monday," I said.

Then Christopher Goodman turned and headed for the door.

I was just about to explain to Mildred my idea for a pain-free piglet project, when suddenly she shrieked and jumped backward.

"What the heck?" I said. "Am I frightening you with my pigs?"

"No, it's not the pigs. It's a rat!" said Mildred. "A rat, sleeping with the alpaca!"

"The alpaca?" I said.

The alpaca was lightly dozing with its legs tucked up under its body. I followed Mildred's eyes, and . . . sure enough, snuggled up in the alpaca's long white wooly coat was a tiny creature. Its ribcage rose and fell with every sleepy breath. But this was no rat.

"It's a dog," I said. "It's that little Chihuahua that was barking at the alpaca earlier today. Remember it? When Hunger first came over looking for poop?"

"I didn't even notice," said Mildred.

"Well, I did," I said. "This dog was barking its little head off. As if that alpaca couldn't stomp him into a little red Chihuahua smear."

"But look at them now," said Mildred. "I guess they made friends. He's so cute." And she crouched to pet the dog, but it snapped at her.

"Hey!" said Mildred. "He's mean."

"He's not mean," I said. "He's injured. See his neck? That collar has rubbed it raw. Looks like he chewed through his leash. Probably got tangled and desperate."

I gave the nervous little fella a couple pellets of goat feed and a dish of water. By then he trusted me enough to remove his collar. I handed the collar to Mildred and applied the same antibiotic ointment I had used on my piglet's tail.

"Okay, sweet pea," I said. "Now let's give you a good brushing."

That's when some kid across the street shouted, "Scrabbles!" And the little dog started barking his head off and wagging his tail.

Leonard Pelf • *The Runaway*

"Scrabbles!" I'm yelling. "Scrabbles!"
And there he is, near the closed up petting zoo.
All them animals are put away except for Scrabbles
with two girls who have set out bowls of food and water.

One girl is small and quiet. The other is big and mean.
The mean girl runs a brush along Scrabbles's back.
And she tries to give me a piece of her mind.

She says, "Hey, little man. You need to take care of your dog.
We found him sleeping in the alpaca pen.
He had no water or food. And his collar was so tight
he's rubbed some of his own skin off.
And he acts half-starved. Has he eaten anything all day?
And you need to brush him.
Even short-hair breeds need the brush."

Lance says, "Mind your own business!"
But I say, "Shut up, Lance. She's right."
Then I say, "Thank you," to the big mean girl.
I tuck Scrabbles under my arm and walk away.

I am so relieved to have found Scrabbles.
But more than ever I want to get away from this town,
this town full of lawyers and losers and liars.
I figure I'll get me one of them dog brushes in Hollywood.
But now, I'll need dog food and the keys to Mr. and Mrs. G's car.

They'll be long asleep by now. Resting up for church.
Dog food will be in the pantry.
Church offering money in the cookie jar.
Car keys hanging on the peg in the kitchen.

Hazel Turner • *The Farm Girl*

The first thing I noticed about this kid was the look of relief on his face at the sight of the little dog.

Good, I thought. *At least the kid cares.*

The second thing I noticed about this kid was the forced smile on his face.

Strange, I thought. *This kid has something to hide.*

The third thing I noticed about this kid was the other kid with him: scowling, defensive, overdressed in a beat-up green army jacket. His right-hand pocket hung lower than the left. Something heavy. Quarters for pinball? A wrench? A gun?

Bad, I thought. *That kid is trouble with a capital T.*

The two boys walked away, and I stepped into the camper to powwow with my parents.

Mildred and me are meeting Hunger for pizza.

Yes. Hunger McCoy.

No. We are not "back together."

No. There's nothing more to say.

Yes. I love you, too.

I was tired from the long day of children and ponies and petting zoo poop. And I was hungry enough to eat a whole alpaca.

"Come on, Mildred. Let's get a move on," I said. "There is a pizza at Mr. Fooz with our names on it!"

"Come on, Mildred. Let's get a move on," Hazel said. "There is a pizza at Mr. Fooz with our names on it!"

And I *did* get a move on, because by then I was starving. Apparently a good girl works up a hunger being bad. I called my mother from the corner pay phone to let her know that I'd be "going out with friends."

Yes, Mom, you heard me right. I'm going out with friends.

No, Mom. None of them are stamp collectors.

Yes, Mom. They are all "normal" kids, same age as me.

Yes, Mom. I love you, too.

And Hazel was rolling her eyes and tapping her watch.

Then I hung up the phone, but we didn't get but half a block when we ran into none other than Christopher Goodman, all by himself. And my heart stopped along with my feet. And I was just standing there.

And Christopher said, "Mildred, where are you off to?"

And I said, "We're going for pizza."

And he said, "Ah, sounds good. I'm on my way home pretty soon. Maybe stop at Carol Lee's for a donut first."

And I wanted to say, *Oh, why don't you come have pizza with us instead?*

But instead what comes out of my mouth is, "Oh." Followed by a squeak.

"Yes," Christopher Goodman says. Silence. Awkward silence.

"Well, then. Enjoy your pizza," Christopher Goodman finally said. "See you later, Hazel."

"Okay," Hazel said.

"Well done, Strawberry," Hazel said as we resumed our walk to Mr. Fooz. She shook her head and closed her eyes. "Well done."

Leonard Pelf • *The Runaway*

Clickety, clickety, clickety, clickety.

Scrabbles's toenails are like water torture.
But we finally reach the trailer park
and I leave him with Lance by the Dumpsters.
Mr. and Mrs. G's trailer is dark and quiet.
So I open the door and walk in, careful as a cat burglar.
Then I make my way to the kitchen
and take the car keys off the peg.
I take the advice of the mean girl from Deadwood Days
by grabbing Scrabbles's food dish and his bag of Gravy Train.
Then just as I'm reaching to lift the lid from the cookie jar,
I drop the bag of dog food all over the floor
loud enough to wake the dead, and then

YIP! YIP-YIP-YIP! YIP-YIP-YIP-YIP!

Suddenly Scrabbles is in the kitchen with me!
And he's barkin' his head off!
And the light clicks on and Mr. G is standing there.
He's in his pajamas and his slippers. And he's pissed off.

"Where you been, kiddo?" he says.
"Did you forget the curfew?"

"Yes sir," I say. "I'm sorry. I was just—"

"Why do you have the dog food, Leonard?" he asks.

"I . . . was . . . just—" I say.

Then Mr. G sees the keys to the Chevy in my hand,
and he starts putting two and two together and says,
"Were you and Scrabbles going for a ride?"

"No," I say. And I smile like Momma taught me.
But the smile ain't workin'. Not at all.

"I don't know what your game is with our car," says Mr. G,
"But you are *not* driving it. Not now. Not ever.
Not until you have cleaned every inch of it!"

By the time Mildred and I got to Mr. Fooz, the place was packed. But Squib and Doc had just gotten us a booth. So far we'd only gotten menus. Hunger hadn't arrived yet. Squib and Doc were across the room playing the new Space Invaders video game. Whoop-de-do!

"Have you ever played Space Invaders?" Mildred asked.

"Hell, no," I said. "I am no great fan of pinball. And video games are even worse. Worst of all is watching some boy play either one. I would rather cut off my arm than sit and watch boys *doing things*: Boys playing football. Boys skateboarding. Boys wrestling. Boys working on cars. Boys acting stupid. Boys talking shit."

"Boys dumping a barrel of shit in the front seat of a Chevy," said Mildred with an evil smile.

"Why, Mildred Penny," I said, looking prim. "Aren't you catty. I've never heard you curse before."

"Well," said Mildred, "I've been hanging out with a bad crowd."

"Well, you *could* be hanging out with Mr. Trombone instead," I teased her. "Why didn't you ask him to join us, back there, when you had a chance?"

"I don't know," she said. "I'm scared."

"Scared of what?" I asked. "Pizza?"

"Well, it's too late now, anyway," Mildred said

"You know where he parked his car, don't you?" I said.

"Yes," she said. "You know I do."

"Well then, write him a note," I suggested. "And leave it on his windshield."

"Won't that seem sort of desperate?" she said.

"I get the impression that Christopher Goodman isn't all that judgmental," I said. "Just write a damn note! Here's a napkin. And I'll bet a million dollars you've got a pen in that old-lady handbag of yours."

"Yes. Of course I do. But—"

"Allow me to dictate," I interrupted. "Dear Mr. Trombone."

Christopher, Mildred wrote instead.

"We are at Mr. Fooz," I went on. "And I *really* want you to come . . . and lick my stamp!"

Join us at Mr. Fooz! Mildred wrote instead.

"Don't keep me waiting. I'm ready for you," I dictated.

Hope you can make it, Mildred wrote instead.

"Lustfully yours, your little Milly Kitten," I said, breathing heavily.

Mildred and Hazel, Mildred wrote instead.

"Beautifully done," I said. "Now all you got to do is deliver it."

"But what if he really doesn't want to come?" she said.

"Then he won't," I said.

"But it would be too embarrassing," she said.

"What would be too embarrassing?" asked Squib, sliding into the booth with Doc. "I know *all* about *fssst* embarrassing!"

"There's a boy Mildred likes," I said. "But she's too shy to tell him."

"Really?" said Doc.

I said, "Mildred, you talk to Doc and Squib without breaking out in hives. What's so different about Mr. Trombone?"

"Who's Mr. Trombone?" asked Doc.

"Doc and Squib are different," said Mildred.

"If you trust Cling and Clang so much," I said, "why not have them deliver the note for you?"

"Really?" she said.

"Sure," I said, rolling my eyes. "It'll be just like we're all still in fourth grade."

"What note?" said Doc.

"She wrote this hot and steamy little note to put on Christopher Goodman's windshield," I said. "Why don't you guys go deliver it?"

"Oh," said Doc.

"Not me," said Squib. "I'm next up at Space Invaders, and I don't want to miss my turn."

"How chivalrous, Squib," I said. Then "How 'bout you, Doc? You know Goodman, right? Why don't you do a girl a favor and deliver that note, so she doesn't have to suffer the indignity."

"Hazel," said Mildred, "I'm sure Doc has better things to do."

"No, no," said Doc. "I'm happy to help out."

"Really?" said Mildred. "Thanks, Doc. I'd really owe you one."

Doc said, "No problem, Mildred. I'm glad to help. I think I know where he parked."

"Uh-oh," said Squib. "Be sure it's the right car this time. Last time he nearly got arrested!"

"Shut up, Squib," said Doc. "I live right across the road from the Goodman's, remember? I see that orange car every day. I think I can manage."

"It's the only orange Ford Maverick next the only ugly

green-and-white Ford Pinto," said Mildred. "Thank you, Doc. Thank you so much."

Finally Doc headed out the door with the note.

"There," I said. "I'm done playing matchmaker. Let's move on to more important things. Like eating." I opened up a menu.

Then, as Mildred was putting her pen back into her old-lady handbag, she suddenly stopped and said, "Hey. Look at this." And she pulled out the dog collar I had removed from the Chihuahua earlier that night. At the time I hadn't examined it. I had been more concerned with the little dog's wound.

"I slipped it in my bag," said Mildred as she read the collar's ID tag. "I forgot all about it."

Then Mildred gave a slight gasp and held her hand to her mouth.

She looked shocked, then confused. "What is it?" I said.

"Read the tag," said Mildred. And she handed me the collar.

Now I gasped, myself, when I read:

My name is

"Scrabbles"

I belong to
Fletcher and Phyllis Grimshaw
3016-F Eagle Street
Goldsburg, VA

Leonard Pelf • *The Runaway*

"I heard Scrabbles barking. What is it? What's happening?"
Now Mrs. G is up in her nightgown—standing in the kitchen.
And Mr. G is talkin' at me, but he's not makin' any sense.

"I don't know what your game is with our car," he says.
"But you are *not* driving it. Not now. Not ever.
Not until you have cleaned every inch of it!
Not until you've paid for every bit of damage."

"What?" I say. "What damage?"

"How could you do this to Mrs. Grimshaw?" he said.
"How could you do this to me? And Miss Hanna?"

"What're you talkin' about?" I felt like I was about to puke.
"I ain't done *nothin'* to you. *Or* your precious car."

"The heck you haven't," says Mr. G. "Some boy named Wayne
dumped it full of manure not two hours ago.
Now *tell* me you had nothing to do with that."

Mrs. G says, "Has that boy, Lance,
got you into some kind of trouble?"

"Manure?" I say. "I got no idea what you're talking about."

"My car is filled up with shit, Leonard!" Mr. G yells.

"And it sure as heck isn't because of *me!*"

"You're accusing me of something I didn't do," I yell back.

"You won't learn your lesson," he says,
"until you face what you've done.
Believe me, I have firsthand experience with you kids."

"It's just a misunderstanding," I say.

"Well, we'll see about that," says Mr. G.
"Now I'm sorry for losing my temper,
but you need to clean up that dog food.
And then you need to get into bed.
You've obviously been drinking. You reek of it.
We'll talk about this after church tomorrow."

Squib had finished his turn at Space Invaders. Hunger had safely delivered his parents home and rushed back downtown to join us. I had returned from my note delivery errand. Finally we were all together in our cozy booth at Mr. Fooz.

To be clear, I had *not* delivered Mildred's note. And I told her Christopher Goodman's orange car was gone by the time I'd gotten to the parking lot. I still had the napkin, neatly folded in my pocket. I imagined Mildred Penny's small, neat lettering. Imagined that the note had been addressed to me. Left on my own windshield. I imagined that I had read it for the first time, and heeded its request.

When I told her that Goodman's car was gone, the disappointment on Mildred's face stung just a little. But I was glad to be there. With Mildred. Mildred and her green eyes. Her green eyes were not looking at Christopher Goodman. They were looking at me.

At first the conversation was all about the dog that Hazel and Mildred had found. How was it possible that the dog belonged to Mr. Self-Righteous himself? What were the odds? And who were the two boys? Did Mr. Self-Righteous have two sons? And what's more, could this dog have been the same little dog that had disrupted the robbery of Squib's ice cream truck just a week ago?

"Perhaps," Squib said, "this is the superposition of Schrödinger's cat in action."

"Oh, God, not the cat again," I said. But he went on.

"You see, the 'many-worlds interpretation' of quantum theory would have us believe that every possible outcome of a situation actually plays out in its own separate reality. *Fssst* Our existence is merely a series of events constantly dividing and subdividing into multiple worlds. At a traffic light, for example, you can choose to turn *left*, but in a separate branch of the universe, you have just turned *right*. Theoretically these two realities will never intersect, *fssst* or be aware of each other's existence."

"Is this leading somewhere?" asked Hazel.

"No," I said. "Trust me."

"But what if something goes wrong?" Squib continued. "What if there are suddenly multiple Chihuahuas and Chevys out there crossing paths? What if life has become like a pinball machine with multiple pinballs, all simultaneously in play, bouncing against one another? Wreaking havoc on reality!"

"What the hell did he just say?" said Hunger.

"It's probably just a coincidence," offered Hazel. "Goldsburg isn't all that big. We're just like crowded pigs in a holding pen. You're bound to get your tail bitten more than once by the same pig."

"What the hell did *she* just say?" said Hunger.

"I'm saying," answered Hazel, "that it's probably just a coincidence."

By way of closing the discussion, Hunger said, "What we need is a lot less serious talk and a lot more serious pizza! But first, I'd like to propose a toast."

We all raised our waters high. Hunger went on.

"To Operation Petting Zoo Poop, and the weirdest crew of co-conspirators a fella could hope for!"

There were cheers all around.

And finally the waitress got to our table. She was dressed in cowboy boots and cutoff jeans, with a toy gun belt slung on her hips. The holster held a bottle of ketchup.

"Sorry for the delay, y'all. I'm your Deadwood Days barmaid, Calamity Jane. Welcome to the Aces and Eights Saloon!"

Leonard Pelf • *The Runaway*

"We'll talk about this after church tomorrow," says Mr. G.

"I ain't goin' to church, tomorrow," I say.
"Me and Scrabbles are goin' to head off on our own.
Now, you and Mrs. G has been good to me.
And I appreciate all—"

"You're not takin'. That dog. Anywhere," says Mr. G.
"Scrabbles is family. How dare you? We trusted you."

"But . . . you told me he was mine to take care of," I say.

"But he's not yours to *have*, Leonard," says Mrs. G.
"Scrabbles is a part of this family. He stays put.
And you are a part of this family too. For better or worse.
We are your legal guardians, and this is your home."
Scrabbles jumps up into Mrs. G's arms, lickin' at her face.
Mrs. G says, "What's happened to his collar?"

I don't have any idea where the damn collar is.
And I'm beginning to feel a pain in my chest,
like that *Alien* movie, with that space creature
squirming—about to erupt from my heart.

Mr. G holds out his hand—palm up.
"I apologize," I say, and I put the keys to the Chevy in his hand.

"Now, you head on to bed, kiddo," says Mr. G.
"We'll figure this all out tomorrow."

"All right," I say, real calm. But I'm screaming inside.
And there's no way I'll spend another day in this place
being told what to do, when to do it, and with who.

So I go back into my bedroom and close the door.
And real quiet, I open up my sock drawer.
And the six bullets click like marbles
as I slide 'em into my pocket.

Squib Kaplan • *The Genius*
Doc Chestnut • *The Sleepwalker*
Hunger McCoy • *The Good Ol' Boy*
Hazel Turner • *The Farm Girl*
Mildred Penny • *The Stamp Collector*

Squib

Howdy, fair barmaid.

I require one large pepperoni pizza.

Doc

You can't eat a whole large pizza of your own.

Squib

Watch me.

Hunger

Come on,

Chestnut.

Squib earned it.

Hazel

He earned it.

Mildred

He *did* earn it.

Squib

I *was* the wheelman.

218

Doc

Okay, fine.

Just remember, someone has to pay the bill.

Hunger

If Squib gets his own.

I want my own, too.

Pepperoni, sausage, hamburger,

hold the vegetables.

Squib

A pizza for every man.

And every man for a pizza!

Doc

Squib! Sit down.

And stop being weird.

Squib

What . . . ?

Hazel

One large pie for the ladies!

Mushroom, onion, and sausage.

Mildred

No. Just a single vegetarian slice for me.

And a side salad with vinaigrette, please.

Doc

I'll take a side salad as well, please.

Squib

Since when do you eat salad, Doc?

Doc

Shut up, Squib.

Squib

What . . . ?

Doc

Just bring me a meatball sub, please.

Squib

Who wants a soda? Sprite for me.

Hunger

PBR for me.

Hazel

Budweiser.

Mildred

Tab, please.

Doc

Uh. Mountain Dew.

Squib
Hey, Hazel. *Fssst*
Can I have some of your beer?

Doc
Squib!

Hazel
No.

Squib
Hey, Hunger.
Can I have some of your beer?

Doc
Squib!

Hunger
No.

Squib
Hey, Mildred.
Did you know that Tab
causes cancer in lab rats?

Doc
Squib!

221

Mildred

I thought that was a myth.

Squib

Well, if you think science is a myth . . .
Anyway, *I* wouldn't drink it.

Mildred

Uh . . .

Doc

Tab is fine, Squib.

Squib

Fine if you like cancer!

Hazel

Squib!

Squib

Oh. Sorry, Hunger. I just get talking. . . .

Hunger

S'all right,
Kaplan.

AWKWARD SILENCE

222

Squib

Tab and Mountain Dew
both contain a *lot* of caffeine.
Caffeine makes me chatty.

Hunger
Oh, really?

Hazel
I can't imagine.

Squib

Forsooth. Absolutely.
Scientific studies have also determined
that Mountain Dew causes
shrunken testicles in—

Doc	Hazel	Mildred	Hunger
Squib!	**Squib!**	**Squib!**	**Squib!**

Squib
What . . . ?

Leonard Pelf • *The Runaway*

"What's going on, Lenny?" says Lance.
"I been waiting by this smelly Dumpster for an hour!"

"It's only been like fifteen minutes, you moron," I say.
"I had to wait for Mr. and Mrs. G to go back to bed."

"I thought maybe you'd chickened out on me," said Lance.

"I'm here, ain't I?" I say.

"Where's the dog food?" says Lance. "Where's the dog?
I tried to keep it with me, but it squirmed away.
I figure it went runnin' back to you in the trailer."

"Scrabbles ain't comin'," I say. "Change of plans.
We're going to California without the dog.
And we can't use Mr. G's Chevy, neither,
'cause someone dumped a bunch of shit in it
as a joke or somethin'."

"Someone dumped shit in Mr. G's car?" said Lance.
"Who would do something like that?"

"Mr. G thinks *you* had something to do with it," I say.
"Probably it was Billy and Dean Harmon mad at us
because we dug up the gun before they could steal it.

But Billy and Dean Harmon can rot in hell
'cause now we've got the gun *and* the bullets."

I fish around in my pocket. Then hold out my hand.
"Here they are," I say. "Now load 'em up."

Lance fumbles the gun open.
One by one he plucks six bullets from my hand.
One by one he slips six bullets into the cylinder.
Then he puts the gun back in his jacket pocket.

"Now," I say, "we are going back to Deadwood Days.
And this time we ain't leavin' without a car."

•11•

THIS GUY MIGHT DO

Deadwood Days
(Sometime Near Midnight)

Leonard Pelf • *The Runaway*

The walk downtown is quiet without Scrabbles's toenails clickin'.
I stop to puke. And that sobers me up . . . a little bit.
We finally get back to Deadwood Days.
The streets are pretty much empty.
Still a few cars left in the Mr. Fooz parking lot.
Looking in car windows. Looking for keys. Jiggling doors.
Jiggling handles. Looking for the easy steal.
It's getting later every minute. The thought of waking up
one more day in this shitty town makes me ill.
What if Mr. and Mrs. G look in to find me gone?
Maybe they'll send the cops looking for me.
Maybe they won't do nothin' at all.

"Hey, Lenny," says Lance. "This guy might do."

And there's this boy, holding a donut, walking to his car.
Maybe it's the drugs, but his bell-bottoms are huge.
So I ask this boy if he'll give us a ride. Just a little ways.
Nothing unusual about that. Two fellas looking for a ride.
And he's kinda nervous and says it's late
and he's gotta get the car home. Home.
I suppose this kid's got a mom and a dad
and a sister and a brother and a real house
instead of a shitty trailer. Who could blame him
for wanting to go home. Anyway, I can tell
he doesn't really want to give us a ride . . . at first.

But then I smile. The smile my momma taught me.
And I tell the boy, "Just a short ride. Promise."
And the boy says, "Okay. Sure. Hop in."

This kid's little car is *not* Bo and Luke's General Lee,
but *You git what you git, and you don't pitch a fit!*
That's what Momma used to say. No matter,
I'm so stoned I can't tell what kind of car it is anyway.

All I know . . . it's orange. It's an orange car.
It's orange like the General Lee.

The conversation at Mr. Fooz was awkward at first, but we warmed up and got into a rhythm. Hazel and Hunger were full of stories of growing up together. Squib kept sipping my Mountain Dew and talking faster and faster about physics and Shetland ponies and the history of pizza. By the end of the night he had charmed us all. And I was actually kind of happy to be his best friend.

From time to time I would catch Mildred Penny's eye and smile. And she would smile back. And when time came to leave, the issue of rides came up. And that's when Mildred Penny asked me if I needed a lift. And I said, "Yes!" perhaps a little too quickly.

Logistically Mildred's offer made sense. Hazel was staying in a camper with her folks. Hunger lived far out of town along the river. Squib lived among the rich folks at the farthest end of Country Club Drive. Mildred was the only one there who could drop me off at my house without having to go out of her way.

Still, I was happy to spend time alone with Mildred, even if it *was* due to logistics rather than romance. But as we walked toward the parking lot I began feeling more and more anxious. And maybe even a bit guilty. I knew I was not Mildred's companion of choice. Her note weighed heavy in my pocket.

Then I saw the empty space where Christopher Goodman's car had once been. And I breathed a little sigh of relief. And that's when I realized that I had been holding my breath almost from the moment I had left Mr. Fooz.

I may as well say it now. If Christopher's car had still been there, Mildred Penny would have known that I had lied when I told her I was unable to deliver her note.

But now there was a second note. This one on Mildred's windshield. A note that hadn't been there before. And she snatched it up. And the smile on her face was a dagger in my heart.

"It's a note from Christopher," Mildred said, blushing.

"Oh, great," I said, trying to smile.

"He says, 'Nice hanging out with you today! See you at band practice on Monday. Be well and . . . yawn-WHEEE!, Christopher Goodman.'"

My newly acquired swagger had blown away in the wind. This is what happens when sleepwalkers cross paths with the waking world.

Now, here I was, alone in a car with the girl that I wanted. Our bellies were full of pizza and our imaginations were full of adventure. As Mildred Penny drove me home, I should have felt giddy. Instead, I just felt like a scumbag.

The only consolation for me that night was the knowledge that I was the only one who knew what I had done. With time perhaps I could actually become the trustworthy friend that Mildred thought I was. And I could forget this ever happened. No harm, no foul.

I made up my mind then and there to give up any romantic intentions toward Mildred Penny. I would consider myself lucky to be her friend. I would enjoy her company without worrying about all the weird head games.

And to this end, as she dropped me off at my driveway, I pointed out Christopher Goodman's house.

"That's where he lives," I said.

"Oh yeah?" said Mildred. "Wow. That's a really nice house."

"Yes," I said. "The houses on that side of the road are all pretty new. Usually Christopher parks his car right there." I pointed at the spot in the Goodman driveway. The spot where the orange car usually was. The spot that stood empty now.

"But I don't see it," I said. "I guess he's gone."

Leonard Pelf • *The Runaway*

The boy plays a song by Queen on the stereo.
Queen ain't bad, but they sure ain't AC/DC.
The boy tells me he's going to listen to this one song
over and over two hundred and fifty times.
Then Lance is in the backseat poking me in the side
trying to hand the gun up between my seat and the door.
He just keeps at it. Poking me with that gun.
Lance is always eggin' me on. He never lets up.

And I tell the boy to go down Ellett Valley Road.
Past the little white church to the wide spot in the road.
And now the music is off and it's dark and quiet.
And the boy's bell-bottoms swish across the road.
And I shove the boy. Or maybe Lance shoves the boy.
And the boy tumbles down the bank.
All hippie sandals and big bell-bottoms.
Old moldy leaves. Dirt. Sticks. He tumbles.
And one sandal goes flyin'. I ask, "Are you all right?"
And he gets to his feet. Replaces the sandal.
And it comforts me to see both sandals on.
And he looks up. Reaches into his pocket.
Hands up his wallet. Arm outstretched and shaking.
Now his hand is empty. More shaking. *Now what?*

Suddenly the boy is scrambling up the bank.
A burst of speed up the steep bank. *Now what?*

I'm sick of all the things I cannot do. *Now what?*

And *POP!* And the boy is spinning. Holding his shoulder.

Now here is something I *can* do. I am in control of this.

And *POP!* And the boy drops.

And I feel

the weight of him drop

through the soles of my feet.

The sound

of a deer when it drops to the ground.

The sound

of the boy through the cotton in my head.

And Lance says, "Come on, Lenny!

Come on.

Let's get out of here!

Come on, Lenny!

Come on!"

•12•

TEACH ME WHAT REMORSE IS

Four Weeks
After
Deadwood Days

Doc Chestnut • *The Sleepwalker*

For a little while, Squib and I were celebrities of a sort, for being the ones who had discovered the body of Christopher Goodman. Because we had been the first to see Christopher Goodman dead, we were approached by many who claimed to be the last to see Christopher Goodman alive. *I saw him playing Space Invaders. I saw him in the donut shop. I saw him listening to music. He told me hello. He told me good-bye. He told me see you later.*

And every storyteller confessed a twinge of guilt. Because everyone (and there were many) who had seen Christopher Goodman at Deadwood Days felt somehow responsible for not stopping the horrible thing that had happened. This horrible thing that had happened right under our noses.

And no one shared more in those feelings of guilt than the five of us who had carried out Operation Petting Zoo Poop. It took a few weeks, but eventually we had all come to realize the connection between Mr. Self-Righteous and the boy who shot Christopher Goodman. And we all learned, firsthand, that we had essentially foiled the young murderer's plan to take Mr. Self-Righteous's car.

Wayne Wilson, who had been left on the hook for the vandalism at the trailer park, found himself tangentially caught up in a murder investigation. Wayne, understandably, spilled his guts. And eventually the police came to call on each one of us.

In the end, Mr. Self-Righteous refused to press charges against us, and the police wrote off the incident as just a prank gone terribly wrong. Still we couldn't help but dwell on how we had helped divert a killer . . . toward Christopher Goodman.

So now, four weeks after Deadwood Days, we sat in Advanced Literacy Studies: Creative Writing, Mrs. Maybury urging us to "mine our grief for literary gems." I felt certain that Mrs. Maybury would have been stunned by the depth and complexity of our grief. She would have been terrified by the weight and clarity of the gems we held locked inside — and the dragons standing guard over the hoard.

Hazel Turner • *The Farm Girl*

Mrs. Maybury wants us to write out our memories of Mr. Trombone. And all I can think of is how nice he was. And how he was so concerned over my piglets. He just came off as different. Not bad or good, just different. Like he knew some secret that no one else knew. He was almost too comfortable, too innocent. But maybe I wouldn't think that way if he hadn't got himself killed.

When Mildred first told me what had happened, it wasn't Christopher Goodman who was on my mind, but the boy who shot him. Truth is, I saw the kid earlier that day looking at the horses. It sticks in my memory because he had that noisy Chihuahua with him. And he studied the horses, standing stock-still, in a trance. He watched the little Shetlands go around and around, and I could tell he felt like me. He looked at the ponies going round in circles and, maybe, he saw himself.

The papers say he was running away to California . . . same as I hope to do. Maybe that kid just wanted out like I want out.

And later that night as I laid into him about the poor Chihuahua, I could tell that he knew I was right. And to be honest I thought he really did care about that little dog. I saw a spark in that boy's face. I saw goodness. But then a couple hours later he shot another boy dead.

Guess I'm not such a good judge of character. Or maybe that boy really *was* a good kid. Maybe he needed someone to step up. I suspected they had a gun. I didn't tell. I could have ended the whole thing right then and there. That's what keeps me up at night.

Why didn't I step up?

I first heard about the murder on Daddy's police scanner. Christopher Goodman dressed funny. And he was a little bit strange. But he was nice. He was a good guy. And I guess that's what got him killed.

Them same boys had asked me for a ride in Wayne's Bronco earlier that day. Did I even consider it? Oh, *hell*, no. Christopher Goodman was nice, but I was just my redneck self. Maybe I *should* have offered those boys a ride. If they had pulled a gun on me, I would have kicked *both* their asses!

I never told nobody about how me and Doc saw them boys just before dark. How Doc said them boys were jiggling handles and looking for keys. The boys were already in jail. I figured it didn't matter. But maybe I should have done something when I had the chance. Maybe I should have kicked that drunk boy's ass. Maybe I could have stopped them right then and there.

But I had been too set on my revenge against Mr. Self-Righteous. And ha! Didn't *that* turn around and bite me on the ass! Mom says I'm "acting out" on account of I'm sad about her being sick. And maybe that's true. I don't know.

Mrs. Maybury wants us to write poems about Goodman, but I think I'll write a country song instead. I've tried counting syllables, but my fingers are too busy pickin' strings. Goodman would have appreciated that. Him and his trombone band and his three-ton hydraulic jack. Him and his hippie pants and his dancing cat. As far as that goes, lately, I'm kind of losing interest in roadkill.

The sad thing about resurrecting roadkill is this: You can

bring a creature back to life, but it'll never grow another day older. You can pose it realistically, but it'll keep that pose forever. I suppose that's the kind of grief stuff that Mrs. Maybury wants to hear. But I think I'll write a country song instead.

Mildred Penny • *The Stamp Collector*

Join us for pizza. Join us for pizza. Join us for pizza.

Four words. It should have been so easy to say. *Hello, Christopher. Join us for pizza.* If only I had had the guts to say it, I'm certain he would be alive right now. Hazel says that's crazy logic, but she has to admit—I could be right. Christopher *might* have been eating pizza at Mr. Fooz, instead of giving rides to boys with guns.

Since Deadwood Days I've returned to my stamps. They are orderly. And quiet. And calming. It makes me feel good to see them in their proper place. I've taken comfort in my complete set of 1932 George Washington Bicentennial stamps. All twelve of them accounted for, thanks to Hazel. One stamp for every phase of Washington's life.

Christopher Goodman should have had a full set too. High school graduate. College student. Famous musician. Father. Imagine all the things he would have done. The people he would have been. There may have been a stamp depicting his life with *me*. Or at least our first date. Is that too much to ask?

I wish I had even a single stamp to place into my book. Christopher Goodman at seventeen. He's been gone barely a month and already I am forgetting what he looked like. How can that be? We had something. Forming between us. It could have lasted a month. A year. A lifetime.

I'm angry. I'm greedy. I'm selfish. And alone. I can't exactly stand up at some memorial and declare, *I am Mildred Penny. None of you have ever heard of me, but I would have been Christopher Goodman's next girlfriend.*

I am not just grieving the loss of a new friend. I am grieving the loss of what might have been. That's what keeps me up nights more than anything else. I don't even have memories to comfort me. All I have is . . . what if.

So now Mrs. Maybury wants us to write about our feelings, and that's good. But an ocean of ink couldn't soothe my sadness. And no stack of process journals is high enough to hide my guilt. *Join us for pizza.* How had it seemed so impossible to say? How could it have been so hard?

Join us for pizza. Had I have been Hazel Turner, I would have said it to his face. Hazel would have tucked him under her arm and carried him off squealing like one of her piglets. But because I was chickenshit Mildred Penny, I held my tongue. And I waited. And I wrote it in a note. And the note was too late.

Christopher Goodman, you absolutely must *join us for pizza.* You must. As if there is no tomorrow. Because maybe there won't be.

It was only four words.

It was only a mouthful of air.

And a life depended on it.

During Deadwood Days Hunger, Hazel, Mildred, Squib, and I had briefly bonded over a common cause — revenge. Now four weeks later, we had bonded over a common sense of guilt. But that collective guilt was nothing compared to the solitary guilt I held hidden in my own heart.

Would Goodman be alive if I had put Mildred's note on his windshield? My imagination constructed every possible scenario. Perhaps Goodman would have driven away without even seeing the note at all. Perhaps the note would have blown away. Perhaps he would have read the note, but refused to join us. Maybe he wasn't interested in Mildred. He didn't like pizza. He had a new curfew. Each rationalization was increasingly absurd.

The note that Christopher Goodman left for Mildred was certainly no torrid confession of love, but it *did* seem to show his appreciation, if not his outright interest. So the likelihood that Goodman would have come to Mr. Fooz at Mildred's invitation was high. At my lowest moments I would lie awake all night, certain that I had killed Christopher Goodman. Other nights I shared the blame with Hunger, Hazel, Mildred, and Squib. And when my heart could bear no more, I would shift the blame to the boy with the gun.

When that boy pulled the trigger, he had turned us *all* into murderers. The motorist who pulled out at just the right time to allow Goodman to fill the space next to Mildred. The baker who insisted Goodman linger a minute for the fresh batch of donuts. The passersby who delayed or hastened his every step. Goodman's lenient father, who refused to impose an early

243

curfew. Even Mrs. Goodman shared the blame by giving life to Goodman in the first place. I comforted myself that we had *all* (in some way) sent Christopher Goodman to his grave. The logic was insane, but it was all I had.

On certain nights, no amount of rationalization or imagination would satisfy my ravenous regret. On these horrible nights none of the rosy scenarios would play in my mind. The only scene left, spinning out in an infinite loop, featured me walking up to Christopher Goodman's car, then turning away as I shoved Mildred's note into my pocket. Over and over again. Take after take after take. Never mind that I had not actually pulled the trigger. On these desperate, rock-bottom nights, I was certain that I was the one who had killed Christopher Goodman.

My name is not really Squib. It's really Scott. When I was in second grade I read that a squib was a tiny explosive charge used in the filming of movies to simulate bullet impacts. So I set out to make my own. I had no access to any actual squibs, so I just taped four or five firecrackers to my T-shirt. Long story short, I came home from the emergency room with second-degree burns and a new nickname. Squibs of various strength have been used by rock miners and road builders for hundreds of years. I bring this up now, because you have to know what a squib is in order to make sense of what I'm about to say.

You see for weeks I tried, and failed, to explain Christopher Goodman's murder algebraically. Then I tried, and failed, to explain Christopher Goodman's murder through the principles of quantum physics.

For a solution I turned to the Famous Squib Case of 1773. And I don't call it famous because it's named after me. It's not. And I don't call it famous because everybody knows about it. They don't. I call it famous because that is actually the name of the case: "the Famous Squib Case of 1773." Somewhere in England a mischief-maker named Shepherd tossed a lit squib into a crowded market. It landed on a stack of fresh fish. The fishmonger, to save himself (and his fish), picked up the squib and tossed it pell-mell back into the crowd, where it landed on a basket of gingerbread and was similarly dealt with by the baker. This time the squib flew into the face of a passerby named Scott, exploding in his face and permanently blinding him in his right eye.

So who was at fault? The first squib tosser? The second? Or the last? The courts found Shepherd, the original tosser, to be the one at fault. That seems like common sense to us in this modern age. But in 1773 things weren't always so fair. I suppose that's why the case is so famous, because it was the birth of common sense. The finger that tips the first domino is guilty, not the dominoes themselves.

So the Famous Squib Case of 1773 tells us that the person who set the chaos in motion must help bear the guilt. But that's little consolation to those of us who become entangled in the chain of events leading up to the final explosion. Had I told the lady cop everything I knew about the ice cream truck robbery, it is possible those boys wouldn't have killed anyone. Did I play my part and "toss the squib"? And how does that make me feel?

I favor facts over feelings. And I would much rather talk than feel. But at the moment, I don't have the slightest idea what I'm talking *about*. None of this talking can explain why that boy pulled the trigger and why Christopher Goodman is dead.

My brain fails me. Reason runs me into walls. I cannot talk my way out of this sadness. I feel as though my soul has been hacked by an ax; I feel as though my soul is just hanging from my body by a flap of skin.

This is not Christopher Goodman's murder. It is ours. It belongs to all of us. It belongs to every single one of us who is left alive.

Leonard Pelf • *The Runaway*

And now the lawyer, Captain Hook,
is on his feet and talking crap again.
Telling the judge all about me, like he knows me so well.
"*Mister Pelf* shows no remorse," he says.
"*Mister Pelf* is not capable of feeling."
Pointing at me with his metal hooky hands.
He talks crazy. I think he really *is* crazy.
The boys in the detention center tell me
one day he found a can of Pringles potato chips
on the roof of his car. And when he went to move it,
it exploded. Blew his hands clean off!
I guess someone out there hated him as much as I do.
Now Captain Hook wants to punish *me*
because some *real* criminal blew off his hands.

Finally Captain Hook sits down.
And Miss Hanna gets up and sets that judge straight.
She lets him know it's not my fault.
Tells him about how I really love animals.
About how I been in a dozen foster homes.
About Momma going to prison because *I turned her in.*
I did the right thing for my little brother and sister.
I took care of them. I got 'em up
and off to school and made them food
and tied their shoes. How I was theirs.
How they were mine. And how we were a family.

Now Mr. and Mrs. G get up and have their say.
They tell the judge I'm really a good kid.
And how I do the dishes and wash the car
and how I stay awake during long Sunday sermons.

Next my court-appointed lawyer begins the blaming.
Now he's blaming my mother and my deadbeat father.
Now he's blaming the grown-ups who bought us beers.
Now he's blaming the stoners for giving us pot.
Blaming Lance's Grandma for not hiding her drugs.
Blaming Lance for having a gun and for egging me on.
Blaming the town of Goldsburg for Deadwood Days.
Blaming Deadwood Days for creating
an "unwholesome atmosphere."

Now the judge asks me what I have to say for myself.
I want to tell him that I'm sorry the boy got shot.
I want to say I wish I woulda let that boy go.
And I wish the police had chased me in that boy's car
so that the police had got shot instead.
I want to tell him, *Teach me what remorse is, and I'll show it.*
But all I say is, "I don't like to get in trouble.
Just seems I always do."

Later that night, the boys in the detention center
tell me that remorse is a fancy word for sorry.

They say I have to act more sad—sorry and sad mixed together.
So I practice it and watch my reflection in a spoon.
"I'm sorry," I say to the spoon.
And it looks like a miniature fun-house mirror.
"I'm *so* sorry. *I'm* so *sorry*. I *am* so sorry."

I am sorry that boy got killed.
I am sorry that boy had a real family that will miss him.
I am sorry that the whole damn town of Goldsburg
is gonna miss that boy 'cause he was so kind and good.
I am sorry the cops took my brother and sister away.
I am sorry nothing ever goes my way.
And I am sorry my hand is all aces and eights.

•13•

THE JUMP

Six Weeks
After
Deadwood Days

Doc Chestnut • *The Sleepwalker*

It took us many weeks to fully realize that Christopher Goodman was gone for good. He would not show up for marching band practice, his elephant bells swishing along the grass. He would not make titanic elephant farts on his trombone. Or jump from the rocks into the New River. Or shout out *Yawn-Wheee!*

He would never form a band of trombones and drums. He would not listen to "Bohemian Rhapsody" two hundred and fifty times. Someone else's initials would eventually mark a new high score on the Space Invaders game. In school Christopher Goodman would not answer roll call. His name would no longer be called at all.

Some people didn't even know who he was. But those who *did* know him had their stories. Every girl had harbored a secret crush. Every boy had envied his easy, fearless way. And everyone who had met him described him as kind. And they would say it with wonder. *He was so kind!* As if his kindness had been a rare condition.

Tuesday, September eleventh, arrived, the day we were due to turn in our Christopher Goodman memorial poems. That morning, just like every morning, I wrote *What's Up? Doc* forty-five times on forty-five copies of the *Goldsburg News Messenger* and delivered them to forty-five houses. The final house, as usual, was the Goodman house, and the paper landed on the wooden front porch with the usual loud bang.

That morning, just like every morning, I put on my running shorts and gathered a set of street clothes and my books for school. Like every other morning Squib pulled up in the ding-a-ling truck and greeted me with a funny little salute.

But unlike every other morning, this morning we had no intention of going for a run. And no intention of going to Creative Writing: Advanced Literacy Studies. No intention of going to school at all.

Instead, as I balanced between the ice cream freezers removing my warm-up pants to reveal a pair of cutoff jeans, Squib pulled up in front of Mildred Penny's house as planned. She climbed into the truck carrying four coffees and a bag of lemon scones, as planned. She wore beat-up sneakers and a two-piece bathing suit under a long T-shirt and tennis shorts, as planned. As planned, under her arm was a large black binder — her precious collection of stamps.

We drove in silence except for Squib's occasional tics. Due to the road's tight curves and the truck's clumsy handling, the drive to the river took a full forty minutes. The sun was up by the time Squib pulled into the parking area of the same grassy clearing (now empty) where the band picnic had been earlier that summer.

As planned, Hunger's pickup truck was there already. Hunger and Hazel standing beside it. Hunger, with an acoustic guitar strapped to his back, wore cutoff jeans and his usual black T-shirt. Hazel wore cutoffs and her blue corduroy FFA jacket.

Mildred handed a coffee to each of us except, of course, Squib. And in silence we walked down the road along the river until we reached the dirty beach clearing. The New River Mailbox was there to greet us, as though it had been waiting. We gathered around it. We ate our scones. We drank our coffees. A curious buzzard flew by to check us out. Then we each pulled out a piece of paper. Each with a copy of the poem we had written and a few words added at the spur of the moment.

Yesterday, we had left copies of our poems for Mrs. Maybury to find on her desk in the morning. Squib, speaking on behalf of our group, had written an introductory note of explanation. We wanted her to have the poems, but it seemed more important that we read them here. Here in this place that Christopher Goodman loved best.

"I'll go first," said Hazel. "This one's for Christopher Goodman." And she read her poem. Then with a nervous laugh, she said, "Ta-da."

"This one's for Christopher Goodman," said Squib. And he read his own poem, without a single tic. Or maybe we had all just stopped noticing.

"This one's for Christopher," I said. And I read my poem, hoping it didn't reveal too much. Hoping it revealed everything.

Then Hunger turned an ear to his guitar and plucked each string as he twisted the tuning pegs. "This one's for Goodman," he said. And he sang his song, eyes closed, from memory.

"This one's for Christopher," said Mildred. And she read her poem in a small, shaky voice. And she cried. But just for a moment. Then, with a clear sense of purpose, she handed us each an envelope, each one preaddressed: *For Christopher Goodman*. Each one fitted with a 1932 George Washington Bicentennial stamp.

"I had to use rubber cement," she said, "to get them all to stick." And we all laughed at that. And we folded our poems and slipped them into the envelopes. And one by one we put them in the New River Mailbox. Mildred shut the little door with a hollow clack. She spun on her heel. And with tears drying on her cheeks, she said, "And now. We jump!"

In half an hour we all stood atop the rock we called the Jump. Hunger's guitar was back in his truck. Mildred's stamp collection was back in the ice cream van. We had all "let our emotions and memories run free within the confines of the prescribed form." And now it was time to pay tribute to Christopher Goodman in Christopher Goodman fashion.

We were already soaked from the wade-out, laughing hysterically along the "safe" way. The water was September early-morning frigid. The soft wind made us shiver. Now we stood atop the Jump still breathing hard from the journey.

Then Squib began to do his insane Squib dance, passing up and down the rock like a duck in a shooting gallery. Then we all joined in. Trying our best not to slip. Laughing. In that wonderful moment, relieved of our grief.

We each had regrets we would live with all our lives. We each had a list of "If Onlys" and "What Ifs." We would make our confessions or remain silent. We would share our guilt with future loved ones or keep it for ourselves. We had each seen Christopher Goodman one final time at Deadwood Days. We had each looked away. And then he was gone. We had the rest of our lives to explain what had no explanation. But today was just for dancing.

Everything around us shone with the memory of Christopher Goodman. The rocks, the snails clinging to the rocks, the clouds, the algae, the river foam, the downstream breeze, the sun beginning to peek through a saddle in the mountains. Christopher Goodman. Forever seventeen. Dressed in outrageous bell-bottoms. His dark hair down to his shoulders. His kind brown eyes. Christopher Goodman, playing elephant farting noises on his trombone. On the bus, arguing over the lyrics of Queen's "Bohemian Rhapsody." Dressed as Paul McCartney on Halloween. In sandaled feet on a summer afternoon, running like mad to fling his thin tanned body into the water.

But now it was Mildred Penny's turn. First and fearless. "Yaaawnnn-WHEEEEEE!" *SPLASH!*

Now it was Hunter McCoy's turn. "Yaaawnnn-WHEEEEEE!" *SPLASH!*

Now Hazel Turner, blue jacket and all. "Yaaawnnn-WHEEEEEE!" *SPLASH!*

And Squib, who would forever be my friend. "Yaaawnnn-WHEEEEEE!" *SPLASH!*

And me. David Oscar Chestnut. Doc to my friends. A sleepwalker, waking up to make the leap. "Yaaawnnn-WHEEEEEE!" *SPLASH!*

The water of the swimming hole was turbulent as we clowned and kicked and flailed and shrieked. Our raucous laughter echoed against the high cliffs. It filled McCoy Falls from bank to bank. Our voices left us behind on their way downstream. Past the rapids. Across the calm water. All the way down to the beach. Where a rusty old mailbox waited in the sedge.

MEMORIAL POEMS
TO CHRISTOPHER GOODMAN

WRITING ASSIGNMENT
Memorial Poem For Christopher Goodman

Write a memorial poem about Christopher Goodman
using iambic pentameter and A/B/A/B rhyme.
Don't worry if you didn't know him very well.
Let your emotions and memories run free
within the confines of the prescribed form!

Include all pre-writing in your process journal.

Due Date: September 11

Dear Mrs. Maybury,

Per your request, find here our completed assignments, turned in on time, by the beginning of class this eleventh day of September in the year 1979. We tried our best to write our poems in iambic pentameter with A/B/A/B rhyme, but they didn't always work out that way. We don't think Christopher Goodman would have minded if the meter was clunky and the rhymes were a little off. (And we really hope you don't mind either.)

Since we have so carefully met nearly every requirement of this assignment, we are hoping you might overlook the fact that we are skipping class today in order to read our final poems at McCoy Falls and to place copies of said poems in the New River Mailbox as our memorial offerings.

With all sincerity (and hope for leniency),

Scott "Squib" Kaplan,
David Oscar Chestnut,
Mildred Penny,
Hazel Turner,
and Hunger McCoy

Dear Goodman,

This here is a real song I wrote. It don't seem quite as good just on paper, so you'll have to take my word that it sounded real good when I sang it to my mom. And wherever you are, if you've got a trombone, the chords of the song are: G, A, and D, with an E-minor or two. Thanks again for helping us get Wayne's Bronco unstuck. From now on I'll be putting a lot more dancing into my taxidermy. I got you to thank for that.

And to tell you the truth, from now on I might spend a lot less time resurrecting roadkill and a lot more time picking the guitar.

I'm very sorry about what happened to you. You really did seem like a good kid.

Later,
Hunger McCoy

COUNTRY SONG POEM

by Hunger McCoy

for Christopher Goodman

I do not give a crap about this poem.
I don't care much for metaphors and rhyme.
But Christopher ain't never comin' home.
And all because, they say, the kid was kind.
I do not give a crap if the meter is all wrong.
I only know that Christopher is gone.
And all he left behind him was a song.

I do not give a crap about this poem.
I don't care much 'bout limericks nor lines.
But Christopher ain't never comin' home.
He was in the wrong damn place at the wrong time.
I do not give a crap if the meter is all wrong.
I only know that Christopher is gone.
And all he left behind him was a song.

Dear Christopher,

I have tried to explain your death algebraically. But there are too many unknowns to solve for. The equation will not balance.

I have tried to explain your death through the principles of quantum physics, but it seems they don't apply. (For a week I even held out hope that you were jumping off rocks in some tangential world that had split off the instant before the bullets hit you.)

Is it God? Did God set up the dominoes and wait for some human to flick the first one? Or is it the opposite way around? Did humans set them up so God could do the flicking? And what about me? Did I set up a domino? And did I flick it? Either way, I'm glad I've got God who is tough enough to withstand my blame and gracious enough to forgive my guilt. I hope you can forgive it too.

Yours,
Squib

THE FACTS

by Squib Kaplan

for Christopher Goodman

I hold out hope that you are still alive
in some invisible parallel dimension.
I also hope this morning's little drive
will not result in after-school suspension.

I find it hard to say the way I feel.
I'm suited best for scientific facts.
Through vigilant review, the facts reveal
I'm sorry you are never coming back.

Dear Christopher Goodman,

I'm sorry if it was bad of me to call you Mr. Trombone. You were so nice. I doubt you minded it. I'm not as nice and kind as you were. I know the kid who shot you had all sorts of troubles of his own. But if I had the opportunity, I would cut off that boy's balls and stick them in my jar with the pigs' testicles. But it isn't up to me. So I'm just sorry you're gone. And I know Mildred Penny is missing you. Next year I mean to start a new FFA project. I'm going to call it Pain-Free Piglets. Ha, ha. All thanks to you.

Yours,
Hazel

TOO NICE

by Hazel Turner

for Christopher Goodman

When I met you I wasn't so impressed.
I've changed my mind, though, now that you are dead.
It wasn't how you looked or how you dressed.
It wasn't what you did or what you said.

The one thing that you always were was nice.
You never put me down or acted tough.
Did kindness, in the end, cost you your life?
Perhaps just being nice just ain't enough.

Dear Christopher,

Hey, you. So I guess that's it? No first date? I try to think of what you would do if the tables were turned and you were in my situation. I try to do that every day. I've been thinking it over a long time now. And I think the first thing you would do is forgive yourself. Which I'm trying very hard to do. Some days are better than others. The second thing you would do is to let go a little. So I hope you like the 1932 George Washington Bicentennial stamp! "Easy come, easy go," right? The last thing I am pretty certain you would do, if you were standing in my shoes, would be to jump off the biggest rock you could find. And shout out "Yawn-WHEE" at the top of your lungs. And make the biggest splash you could.

So this one's for you. Thanks for everything.

Love, love, love,
Mildred

NEVER

by Mildred Penny

for Christopher Goodman

I'll never get to tell you how I feel.
I'll never get to hear your awful band.
I'll never know if what we had was real.
I'll never even get to hold your hand.

We'll never get to savor our first kiss.
We'll never get to watch our friendship grow.
But worse than all the nevers that I'll miss;
No other soul on Earth will ever know.

Dear Christopher Goodman,

What's up?

Doc

THE WHAT, THE WHERE, THE HOW, THE WHO
by Doc Chestnut

for Christopher Goodman

The papers tell the tale of Deadwood Days.
They tell the what, the where, the how, the who:
you died; back road; a gun; two runaways.
I've read the facts, but still don't have a clue.
Am I to blame for what happened to you?

I'm told, with time the memory will fade.
I didn't pull the trigger; that is true.
I try, but can't deny the part I played.
I know the facts, but still don't have a clue.
Am I to blame for what happened to you?

AUTHOR'S NOTE

When I was a sophomore at Blacksburg High School in southwest Virginia, Edward Disney moved with his parents into a house across the street. He was a great kid. He played trombone in the marching band. He made a lot of friends. Then a year and a half later, on a Saturday night, he reluctantly gave two boys a ride home from the Deadwood Days street festival. The younger of these two boys produced a gun and told Ed to drive down a secluded road. That same boy then forced Ed out of the car, pushed him down a bank, and shot him twice, once in the back, once in the head. The killers drove Ed's car north on I-81 as far as Staunton, Virginia. They removed about thirty dollars from Ed's wallet and then tossed it out the window as they passed Roanoke. Not long after that they pulled into a restaurant parking lot and fell asleep. And that's how police officers discovered them, quite by accident, the next day. The boys had killed Ed for his car and driven it less than a hundred miles. Ed was seventeen years old. The boy who pulled the trigger was only fifteen.

The murder of Edward Charles Disney was a shock to the whole town. Deadwood Days was canceled the next summer out of respect, and it was never held again. There was no funeral. The marching band had a makeshift memorial during band camp, but those of us who grieved his loss were mostly left to twist in the wind.

Keith Moon, drummer for The Who, had died the summer before. Elvis had died the summer before that. But Ed had been a kid. And one of us. We rode the same bus. We were both in marching band. I was Ed's friend but certainly not his *best* friend. He was an upperclassman. We moved in separate circles. Others had known him better.

Yet as the years passed I couldn't get Ed out of my mind. And that I hadn't been very close to Ed seemed only to worsen my obsession. At some point I began returning to Blacksburg around the anniversary of Ed's death. Deadwood Days had been resurrected and reinvented in 1981 as Steppin' Out, a more family-friendly affair. But each summer, around the time of the festival, I would bypass the bustle of downtown and head instead to the big diving rock on the New River. That's where I would pay my proper respect to the memory of Ed Disney.

And I still make the annual journey. Usually I'm joined by one or two old friends. We rendezvous on that rock like clockwork. We stand for a moment and think about Ed, and as we take that first jump of the day, we call out "Ed Disney!" all the way down. Why jump off a rock to remember a friend? My first memory of Ed is watching him from across the street attempting to jump over a large landscaping boulder in his front yard. He would take a running start, barefoot, his big bell-bottoms swishing, and he would attempt to jump the rock. Over and over. But he never once cleared it. I like to think that each summer I'm helping Ed Disney to complete the leap.

After twenty-some years of this, it occurred to me that it would make a good book. A group of teens trying to come to terms with the sudden violent death of a boy they had only known in passing.

History is one-tenth what happened and nine-tenths who's tellin' it. Writers of historical novels use fiction to draw the reader more completely into the historical reality of a moment. In *Who Killed Christopher Goodman?*, I have used fiction just as much to insulate myself against the painful intimacy of the memory. Kind of like wearing an oven mitt to hold a hot skillet. I did not write this book to detail the facts of Ed Disney's death. I wrote this book to explore how his death affected those of us left behind.

Enough with the mumbo-jumbo, Allan! I hear you saying. *Just tell us what parts of the story are made up and what parts really happened!*

I'll start with the fiction. The whole "yawn-WHEE" thing is made up, but it is absolutely something that Ed Disney might have said. His friends report he had a fondness for wordplay. Scrabbles the dog is fiction. The ice cream truck robbery is fiction. The various notes left on various windshields are fiction. Mr. and Mrs. G are entirely fictional, as is Operation Petting Zoo Poop. And while there is no New River Mailbox, it *is* inspired by the real Kindred Spirits Mailbox located on Bird Island, near Sunset Beach, North Carolina.

Now on to the factual. A real flesh-and-blood friend of mine, Edward Charles Disney, was shot by two runaways. Ed Disney really *was* a rather remarkable, well-liked fellow. Depending on whom you ask, Ed was either shy or outrageous. His elephant bells were short-lived; he got such flack that he soon changed his wardrobe to blend in. The real Ed Disney was good-looking, with straight dark hair and piercing brown eyes. Most of the women I interviewed admitted to having had a crush on him. He had a passion for music, especially the Beatles. And he really did spend a lot of time scrutinizing the words of Queen's "Bohemian

Rhapsody." He was trusted by his parents and had no curfew.

Doc is mostly based on me as a kid. Squib, Mildred, Hunger, and Hazel are all composites of many, many folks I've known.

I really did deliver newspapers. And the incident in which I was mistaken as a car thief happened to me just as it happened in the book, except the cars in question were two identical Volkswagen Beetles. I plotted my revenge (it involved the carcass of a rotting skunk), but I never followed through with it. The Deadwood Days street festival, held from 1976 through 1979, was just as I've depicted it here, although I have embellished the petting zoo and the taxidermy booths. The Draper Mile is an actual race that I used to run (and still sometimes do). Yes, I really was a runner. And yes, our coach really did have us do LSD workouts over the summer. The Bronco Brothers really existed. And one of my favorite high school English teachers was really named Mrs. Maybury.

Although the names are made up, my depictions of Leonard Pelf and his accomplice, Lance, as well as the details of their crime, are based on newspaper articles and court documents related to the case. The real boy who shot Ed Disney on August 5, 1979, had been in the foster care system. He was tried as an adult and sentenced to forty-one years. He was paroled after serving thirteen years, but was back in jail within the year for other violent crimes. He is now serving three consecutive life sentences.

Ed Disney had many close and dear friends. My heart goes out to you all. You have suffered sorrows that eclipse my own. And I know that many of you have felt guilt. You each suspect you were the last to see him alive, and you regret that you didn't stop him somehow. Make him linger. You could have asked him the time. You could have bumped him. Caused him to go left instead of right. You could have asked him to join you for pizza. Whatever it would have taken to change that horrible course he was on. The memory of Ed's kindness, and your continual love for him, make your grief that much deeper.

Now hear this! I have written this book to let you know, without a doubt, that it is not your fault. You are not to blame. I hereby release you from your burdensome guilt. If this revelation makes you feel happy, then good for you. But if you find you are still sad, well, that's okay too. Maybe we're not here in order to feel good. Maybe we're here to pursue some higher purpose. But at least you can let go of the guilt. And for those of you who find yourself surrounded, still, by that fog of despondency, I hope at least I've given you a little clarity. A tiny bit of light.

Allan Wolf
April 20, 2016

ACKNOWLEDGMENTS

For sharing your memories and thoughts, thanks to John Costain, Elaine Guzmich, Greg Keys, Steve Knoll, Kirsten Miles, Kathy Ross Moore, Mickey O'Neil, Laura Wierwille Schano, Sandra Jean Short-Steiss, George Teekell, Jeff Weidhaas, and Eric Wolf. Then of course Randolph Thomas, Lynn Hill, and especially David Burleson. David wrote me a heartfelt and thorough remembrance of Ed Disney that is, in itself, a priceless literary tribute. Special thanks to my eleventh grade English teacher, Shirley Maybury Egan. To Elizabeth Wills, philatelist and life-long, loyal friend, I am heartbroken that you did not live to see this book in print.

Special thanks to Ed Disney's sisters, Dr. Lynn Disney and Ms. Carrie Disney. And to the rock-jumping crew—past, present, and future—who make the pilgrimage to the rock each summer.

For providing places to write and research: Dr. Bob Hanna; Alice Cohen and Roscoe (the erudite dog); Klaus and Susan Spies; Nikki (the cultured kitty); the Ramsey Library at the University of North Carolina at Asheville; Virginia Tech's microfiche stacks in Blacksburg; the Montgomery County Courthouse in Christiansburg, Virginia; and the magical West Wolf Imaginarium.

For reading early drafts: Peter and Kathryn Graham, Michael Platz, Laurie Wolf, Simon Wolf, Evy Mitchell, and especially the insightful Don Silver. And those who took it from there, including copyeditor/ninja Maya Packard and all the "imaginicians" at Candlewick Press: Maggie Deslaurier for her copyediting review, Martha Dwyer for her incredible proofread, Andie Krawczyk for the inspired subtitle, designer Sherry Fatla, and Elizabeth Bicknell and Katie Cunningham. These last two amazing, talented editors could transform a cold bowl of grits into a transcendent work of literature. I do not have enough x's and o's.

Always and forever, thank you James, Ether, Si, and Ginger.

I've heard from so many, many people over the years as I worked on this book. I apologize if I've left anyone out. I appreciate you sharing your stories with me.

DISCUSSION QUESTIONS

1. Even though we know what's coming, the outcome can be difficult to accept. Were there any points where you found yourself thinking perhaps Christopher wouldn't be killed? What moments had you hoping the inevitable wouldn't actually occur?

2. Mildred, Doc, Squib, Hazel, and Hunger all believe they are partly to blame for Christopher's murder. Do you agree with any of them?

3. So many minor aspects of the story could have occurred only slightly differently and completely changed the outcome. Can you think of any moments you might consider turning points, when there was no going back from the fate laid out for Christopher?

4. Imagine if Doc alone told the full story, or Mildred, or one of the others. How might the story—and your reaction to it—change in each case?

5. What will be the biggest changes in each character after the events of Deadwood Days? How do you predict Christopher's death might affect the behavior and worldview of Mildred, Hazel, Hunger, Doc, Squib, and Leonard through their next few years and into adulthood?

6. Mr. and Mrs. G prove that proclaiming to be devout and righteous isn't the same as actually being good Samaritans. Why are their attitudes and their brand of indifference particularly insidious?

7. How much of Leonard's behavior is because of who he is as a person and how much is due to his unfair upbringing in the foster care system? Can either element be considered independently from the other?